A Cold Winter
With
A
Hot Boy

BY: S.Yvonne

Interested in keeping up with more releases from S.Yvonne? To be notified first of all upcoming releases, exclusive sneak peaks, and contest to win prizes. Please subscribe to her mailing list by texting Syvonnepresents to 22828

Please feel free to connect with me on social media as well:
Facebook: Author Syvonne Powell
Facebook: Author S.Yvonne
Facebook VIP Readers Group:
https://www.facebook.com/groups/5068827261
57516/?ref=share
Instagram: Authoress_s.yvonne

Chapter One
Armani Sincere

"Happy birthday to you. Happy birthday to you. Happy birthday dear Maniiii. Happy birthday to you!" My entire family and my friends sang around me as my eyes lit up at the sparkles flying from the top of my three tier Chanel cake made up of Swarovski Crystals and all of my favorite colors. At the very top, there were exactly seventeen candles, for seventeen years of life. I cheesed from ear-to-ear before blowing out my candles. My daddy stood on the right side of me, and on the right side of him was my stepmother Chantel. She always tried to wear a smile on the outside when she was around me, but I couldn't help but looking at her like she had two heads because she did. She had 'snake' written all over her from the day I met her five years ago.

My daddy was an OG in the game and with her only being five years older than me, and him being twice the age of her, I didn't have to be grown yet to know she only wanted his money. I couldn't stand Chantel because I always had the feeling that she didn't want me around. If she could have my daddy to herself, she would. She didn't work, didn't go to school, didn't cook, didn't clean, but somehow, he still managed to put a ring on her finger. I had come to the conclusion long ago that my daddy wasn't interested in what she had to offer because he didn't need shit from her. She was simply some nice eye candy to have on his arm. I often wished that my real mama was still alive cause I knew for sure my daddy wouldn't have ever left her. Unfortunately, I didn't even get to meet her because she died while having me and like the man he was, my daddy stepped up and did what he had to do. Up until Chantel came in the picture, I had seen plenty of females come and go over the years, so I was used to hoes being around.

It was never my business to get into his shenanigans. However, it was something about her ass that he just kept bringing her around until she wore him down. I was sure she had somebody to put some kind of spell on his ass. Even now, although I was happy to be in this beautiful hall that he had rented out for my birthday, while celebrating with all of these people, I couldn't help but to think about the money that he had spent on it. My daddy treated me like I didn't have ears in the house and lately, I knew he had been running into some money issues with some big people in whatever business he was into because I really wasn't sure. He never told me exactly what he did as if his job was some top agent secret or something. All of my life he had been in and out of town. He never let niggas come to the house, and whenever he was home, he was in the office with the door closed.

I had a feeling that my daddy was some kind of drug dealer, however, I couldn't put my finger on it because he never told me or let me see shit indicating that. I mean, I would hear little shit here and there in the streets, but whenever I asked him about it, his response was always the same; *believe what you see, and none of which you hear.* For that reason, I always left it alone. Besides, I loved my daddy so it wasn't shit he could do wrong in my eyes. I had everything that not even half of the kids my age could get access to or be blessed enough to have. "I hope you wished for more blessings, health, and an abundance of financial wealth. Happy birthday Mani baby." My daddy's deep voice tickled my ear. "Come outside, I have one more surprise for you."

Before I could respond, the DJ was making the announcement for everyone to walk outside. "Bitch what the hell going on?" My best friend Zayla yelled in my ear over the loud music. All of the thugs from my school and the hot ass girls who were with them already had their phones out ready to record knowing that my daddy was about to do it big for me. I didn't have to be outside yet to know that he had copped me a whip. What I wasn't ready for was the brand-new Range Rover Sport wrapped in Matte black. The rims on it matched the truck and the panoramic sunroof was everything. "Omggggg!" Zayla ran to the truck like it was hers and immediately started posing, taking selfies in front of it. I couldn't do shit but laugh at her. I hopped in my daddy's arms and gave him a big ole hug.

"Thank you dadddyyyy." I sang.

He looked at me with the same exact eyes as mine and gave me that look. "Don't fuck this shit up Mani. I'm for real. Handle ya business but be smart. You fuck this one up and that's it." He warned before kissing me on the forehead. I knew he was probably hesitant about this because I had already wrecked the Mercedes that I had, fucking around with Zayla and Tricia after we did some dumb shit trying to be grown and got drunk as fuck one night. My daddy was fine as hell, and although his eyes were on me, I could feel multiple eyes on him. Chantel's was one of them. The fact that he spoiled me burned her bitter ass up inside.

"I won't daddy." I let him know kissing his cheek. I don't know what it was, but something made me want to hug him again as if it would be the last time. Call it an intuition, or maybe we were just bonded like that, but I just knew something didn't feel right. Instead of addressing it, I enjoyed checking out my truck. Everyone was surrounding me taking pictures and videos on the outside and inside of my truck. "I love it so much." I squealed to everyone.

Chantel walked over to me with her phony ass. Her light skin was flawless, and she had her makeup done by the best of the best. The Chanel outfit she wore along with the ice around her neck and on her fingers just screamed 'money.' Her perfectly sculptured body had all of the boys my age drooling out the mouth. If they only knew, they didn't have shit that she was interested in if it wasn't about a dollar bill. "Cute truck." She said dryly. She could've kept that shit. I barely acknowledged her when I rolled my eyes and replied.

"Thanks, but you don't have to keep playing these games with me. You don't like me and never did. You probably secretly hate that he gave me this truck."

She pierced her lips together like she wanted to say some crazy shit to me. With my daddy here, she knew better than that. "Listen, I don't want to beef with you no more, Mani. You feel how you feel and so do I. You think I'm a gold digger and I think you're a spoiled ass little brat. At the end of the day, I'm still glad you had a happy seventeenth birthday."

I took a deep breath and exhaled. "Right. You want to wave white flags now. I get it. Okay, cool. Thanks for the birthday wishes."

I put my focus back on my ride while trying to ignore that unsettling and uneasy feeling that I had in my stomach. I knew I wasn't tripping. Anytime that I felt something in the pit of my stomach, it almost always meant something was about to happen. With all of the commotion around me, I sat in the driver seat blocking everything out until I heard Zayla yelling my name. "Mani! Mani!" She shook me and then snapped her fingers in my face.

I blinked a few times coming back to. "Huh? What happened?"

She frowned. "Lock the doors and let's go back inside cause you're here, but you're not here. Hell, we're having more fun then you."

I agreed with her, just wanting this shit to go away. Slowly hopping out of the truck; I locked it and walked back inside into the flashing lights and loud music. All the while, my eyes focused on my daddy and his crew by the bar. He locked eyes with me and smiled. Even from a distance, I knew they were all strapped. I even knew that it was more than just drinks behind the bar as well. I was sure it was more guns, even bigger guns. I knew he wouldn't have had me this big ass party without any protection around.

"Bitchhhhh!" Zayla squealed looking like a damn cockroach that was bucking from being sprayed while she tried desperately to twerk. She looked back at her ass. "Is it moving?" She asked waiting for our homegirl Tricia to reply, because I knew damn well she wasn't waiting for me to reply. I was tired of watching her non-dancing ass. She finally gave up and grabbed the bottom of her back. "Fuck this shit, I'll work on my Meg the Stallion knees another time cause I'm about to die trying to keep up with her ass." She pouted flopping down on the barstool next to me. She grabbed a soda and popped it open.

Tricia shook her head and laughed. "Just give up all around the board cause ya ass can't dance Zayla, which is a damn shame cause you toting all that ass for nothing."

Blocking them two out, I scrolled my phone with my mouth twisted up looking at all the ridiculous pictures of prom dresses Chantel's ass sent to my phone earlier knowing damn well none of this shit was my style. She knew had I been her biological daughter, she would've never sent me no shit like what she had been sending. Hell, we weren't that far apart in age and she knew this was some stuff she wouldn't have been caught dead in. I locked my phone back and rolled my eyes looking up just in time to see a red beam light bouncing around the hall. "Look at that." I pointed trying to keep up with it. It was coming from somewhere on the second level. "What the hell is that?" I asked Tricia and Zayla just as it landed right on me.

"MANI!" My daddy's voice yelled from across the hall and before I could look to see where he was calling me from, I was being tussled to the ground just as the bullets rang out in the hall.

Blap! Blap! Blap!

I hit my head hard when I fell, but Beano, my daddy's right-hand man wouldn't let me get up. He forced all of his weight on top of me shielding me from bullets as I screamed to the top of my lungs trying desperately to use my eyes to search the hall for my daddy.

"Stay down Mani!" Beano groaned in my ear, but I could tell something was wrong, very wrong. Beano didn't even sound normal. He sounded like he was in pain. I squeezed my eyes shut until the ringing in my ears stopped. When I no longer heard the bullets, I tried to get up again. People were still scramming and running. The DJ didn't even have time to stop the music, because I'm sure he had to hide for cover and dodge bullets, so the music was still going.

"Beano! They stopped shooting! I have to find my daddy!" I cried trying to push his big body off of me. "Beano!" I cried out trying to roll him off of me and wouldn't stop until I was successful. When I realized that he wasn't breathing and my hands were now full of his blood, I almost fainted looking at the first dead body I'd ever seen in my life. His lifeless eyes stared back at me. The tears ran down my face as my body trembled while still on the ground scooting away from him. My eyes bounced around the room trying desperately to spot everyone else until they landed on Zayla's lifeless body. From the side of her head, she was bleeding. The vomit immediately built up in my throat. "Zaylaaaa!" I scooted toward her and hovered over her body crying.

Zayla wasn't breathing and everyone around us was running for their own lives stepping over us both although the shooting had stopped. The tears fell from my eyes to her face as I clung on to her body. Her clammy skin was warm and outside of the gun wound her pretty face looked as if she was simply sleeping but I knew better. Zayla and me had been best friends since the sandbox and we did everything together. There was no me without her. "Zayla, please!" I cried rocking back and forth. "Please wake up, Zayla!" I screamed from the pit of my soul. "I'm so sorryyyy." Rocking back and forth, I whimpered with snot running from my nose and all. It hurt me because she shouldn't have been the one laying here dead.

As bad as I wanted to stay with her, I knew that I couldn't stay. I kissed her forehead with trembling lips and crawled on all fours trying to find my daddy once again. I was almost to the back exit when out of nowhere something was being thrown over my head and I was being lifted in the air. I tried so hard to fight and scream as everything went black and I couldn't see shit. Whatever was over my head was making it really hard and must've had some kind of chemicals in it and slowly, I felt as if my body was giving up before I passed out.

When I woke up, I was in excruciating pain and whatever was over my head was still there. I tried to make a move but that's when I realized that whatever I was laying on, I was bound to it and couldn't move at all. "AHHHHHH! SOMEBODY HELP ME!" I panicked praying like hell that somebody would hear me. "HELPPPPP!"

"Shut up! Just stop yelling before you get us killed!" Another voice whispered causing me to jump because I didn't realize someone was here with me.

"Chantel?" I asked confused.

"Mani?" She asked. "Oh my God, Mani? Is that you?" She sniffed.

I hated her ass, but glad that I wasn't alone. "Chantel! I can't see shit. I can't move!" I whined. "What's going on??"

"Shhhh." She ordered again. "Me either Mani. I can't see shit at all. They got me while I tried to go to the bar and grab a gun." She cried.

"Chantel... who? Who are these people? What the fuck do they want?"

"I don't know Mani. I don't know. I only know we better do what they say if we want to get out of this alive." She warned. I could tell she was trying to be strong, but she was just as scared as me. From above of we could both hear heavy footsteps in a distance until they were closing in on us. My heart was beating fast as hell as the tears burned my eyes.

"Omg Chantel, they are coming back. Where's my daddy?" I cried. "Probably looking for us. I hope he's looking for us." She replied fearful just as the door was unlocking and opening. "Listen! Whatever you want, I'll give it to you. My man has money just don't hurt her! She's just a baby!" I could hear her begging.

Here it was we didn't even get along and she was pleading for my life for me. I could almost hear my heart, that's how loud it was beating. "Shut up bitch." The dude mumbled and I knew that was a voice I didn't even recognize at all.

I knew the best thing for me to do was shut up and Chantel did as well because she wasn't talking anymore. The dude got on the phone and made a call. "Yeah, so what you want me to do with them? Yeah, I got the wife and the daughter. That nigga definitely has to be sent a message." He said and as sure as those words left his mouth, I knew it was over and whatever this was about wasn't even about us, it was about my daddy but the love that I had for him, I would take a bullet for him if I had to. As afraid as I was before he walked in, a sense of calmness overcame me. I knew I would never rat on my daddy. I don't give a fuck what he did. I may have been afraid, but he didn't raise a pussy ass bitch. I wasn't a snitch either, especially not to the man that gave me life. A good one at that. I couldn't hear what the person on the other end was saying, but I heard what the dude around us was saying. "Look, you want to pop the lil one you gotta do that on yo' own. I don't kill no fuckin' kids."

Chantel immediately broke down. "If you gon' kill me then do it nigga. I done seen everything but God anyway. We all gotta go one day! Just do it." She told him. I could tell she didn't mean it, but she had to be strong. I lay here in silence as my little heart hurt for her. I was just getting ready to help plead for her life when a single bullet was shot. *Pow!*

My shoulders jumped. "Ahhhh!" I yelled knowing that he had shot her. "Chantel! Chantel!" I called her name. Nothing, just silence. The dude must've walked away because I heard the door locking again. I couldn't stop the vomit that came up causing me to almost choke on it. As much as I hated her in life, she had gone out like a true 'G' and I prayed like hell I could be that strong when it was my time. This was the beginning of the winter, and I already knew that it was about to be the coldest winter ever if I lived through it. The longer I was tied to whatever they had me lying on, the longer I felt like I was in the sunken place. The dryer my mouth became, the more nauseous I got, and although I fought so hard to keep my eyes open, after many more hours, I succumbed to the back of my eyelids, and not because they were forced shut because of something being tied around my eyes, but because I just simply couldn't take this agony no more.

~ ~ ~ ~

I didn't know how long I was sleep, but when I finally did come back to, I was freezing and

15

shaking while gasping for air. The nightmare that I had envision so clearly Chantel being shot and killed as if I actually seen it. In my mind, blood was probably splattered all over me and this room that I was being held captive in. I couldn't take being in here any longer. If they were gon' kill me, I would rather them had done it now instead of torturing me like this. On top of that, I had to pee so badly and didn't think I could hold it much longer.

"Hello! Can you motherfuckers hear me! Hello!" I yelled as loud as I could. I paused and waited to see if I could hear anything but I couldn't hear shit at all, so I started again deciding that I'd keep going until my voice was gone if I had to. "Hello! You big, fat, funky motherfuckers can hear me! I know you're close because I can smell you!" I carried on figuring if I started insulting them I could get some results.

I don't know if that hit a nerve or what, but my heart started racing when I heard the heavy footsteps closing in on me. Suddenly I almost regretted talking shit but like I said, I wasn't raised to be no pussy. The door swung open and I could feel a rush of cold air come along with it. "You got a smart ass mouth for a young bitch. You ain't scared to talk like that?"

I didn't know the voice, but it wasn't the guy who shot Chantel. "I have to pee." I mumbled. "Unless you want me to pee all over your stuff." On the inside, my heart was about to beat through my chest but on the outside, I tried to be cool. "And why do I have to be afraid? If you wanted me dead, I would be dead right now."

I felt him standing right over me and he smelled just like the outside sun mixed with cologne. Next thing I knew, a strong hand was untying me. "If you try one thing, I'm gon' blow yo fucking brains out right along with this dead bitch over here. Now get up." He forcefully grabbed my forearm holding me up since my legs felt like spaghetti noodles as wobbly as they were. I almost forgot that I'd been in here next to a dead body. "I don't gotta kill you shorty. Boss man got something much better planned for you to pay off that debt ya bitch ass daddy owes."

"What the fuck?" I whispered. My mind was racing as I tried to think fast while being led up some stairs wishing that he would just take the blindfold off of me. He was a big, strong man so I knew I couldn't beat him. If I ran, he might shoot me. If I tried kicking him in his dick and running, I wouldn't even know where I was going so, I had to play it cool and coach myself. Maybe, just maybe everything would work itself out. The entire way he was leading me to wherever I was going, he was antagonizing me.

"You a pretty lil bitch too. We gon' make a lot of money off of you shorty; with yo lil pretty ass."

I swallowed hard and ignored him because I didn't know what the hell he was talking about. I didn't know how to sell no dope and I wasn't a fucking maid nor a mule, so I honestly didn't know what he meant by that. I just wanted to see my daddy so whatever it took right now, I would deal with. We came to a sudden stop and then he knocked on the door in front of us. I could tell it was one of those expensive oak wood doors or something like that based off of the sound. You could always tell the quality of a door when you knocked on it. It slowly opened and he led me inside. "Take the blindfold off." Another male's voice ordered. He was another voice I didn't recognize. Slowly, my eyes were being uncovered and my eyeballs hurt so badly trying to adjust to the outside sunlight shining in through the curtains.

The office space that I stood in didn't look like much, but the man in front of me smoking on a fat cigar did. I had to blink a few times before getting a good look at him while the dude who walked me inside held a gun to the side of my head. Just looking at the cold steel pointed at me had me about to piss on myself. "Take the gun away from her head, she ain't gon' do nothing stupid; ain't that right Mani?" He asked with a crinkle in between his thick brows. His caramel complexion skin was smooth with the exception of the long scar going down the side of his face. He was dressed in a smoked charcoal grey Thom Sweeny suit. His bald head was shiny, and his face was bare. His dark hazel eyes pierced right through me. Although good looking, he looked scary as hell because of that scar. It looked like somebody took a razor blade and sliced his shit open or something. I didn't know the details, but the fact that it healed with a keloid didn't make it any better.

"Where's my daddy?" I asked giving him a cold glare.

He let out a thick cloud of smoke and exhaled. "Don't worry about that. If you wanna see him again, you'll do what I say. Giving me problems is only gon' make it worse." He replied walking around me looking me up and down. Just the sound of his voice caused me to shutter in fear of him. It's like his entire presence demanded respect. He was tall as hell, so he towered over my even five foot frame. If I had to call out his weight, I'd say a solid 250 of merely muscle. His height about six foot two and his age, probably mid 40's or 50's. On his ring finger he wore an iced-out wedding band, which let me know that he had a wife somewhere.

I sucked my teeth and tried not to look too timid. "I don't have nothing to do with shit my daddy got going on but if you think I'm gon' flake on him, you might as well kill me now."

He smirked. "Feisty one huh?" Using his forefinger, he lifted a piece of my hair from my shoulder causing me to cringle. "You don't have to flake on him, you gon' help him live by paying off his tab. That's the only way you'll see that nigga again."

Tired of the small talk, I'd do anything to see my daddy again. I didn't know what he did, but I was willing to do whatever it took to get to him. "If you think he ain't looking for me, you got another thing coming and when he does, he gon' fuck you up."

They both thought that was funny, I wanted to add another scar to the other side of his face and then turn around and drop this big mu'fucker standing behind me, but I knew I couldn't win. "Lil girl you got a lot to learn, but since you think you a woman, we gon' find out. Ya pops owes me a hella tab for some badddd business. You play with my dope; you play with my life cause now you fuckin' with how I feed my family."

Shifting from one leg to the other, I was tired of the small talk and ready to get this over with. "What do you want me to do? Where's the work? I don't know how to push dope, but I can tie the lil baggies and shit."

Scarface, since that's the name I made up for his ass, looked at me without an expression. He then pulled a zip-tie from his drawer and tied my hands back behind my back. Again, I wanted to fight, but I knew better. Scarface then told Big Bird behind me, "cover her eyes back up and take her to the brothel to get cleaned up." Without another word, he walked out excusing himself. Big Bird gave me a lustful look before covering my eyes again. On the way out I kept replaying the word 'Brothel' in my mind wondering where I'd heard it from or what it even meant. As soon as my ass hit the seat of whatever kind of vehicle, he had me locked in as we drove, it hit me like a ton of bricks. I started wilding the fuck out. "LET ME THE FUCK OUT! SOMEBODY HELP ME PLEASE! HELP ME! HE'S GON' KILL ME!"

Whap!

A heavy hand hit my face so hard I heard ringing in my ears. "Can't nobody hear you and can't nobody see you behind these dark ass tints.

Shut the fuck up or next time it's gon' be yo teeth on the floor." He warned.

I swallowed hard not wanting to get hit again, although I had rather to be dead then to do what they were planning to do with me. Now it all made sense, these niggas were about to try to trick me out to pay off a tab that I didn't even owe and who knew how long it would take to even pay it off. I silently prayed hoping that my daddy was okay and looking for me before these niggas ripped me of my soul.

Chapter Two
Mani

A Few Weeks Later

"Ahhh!" The fat nigga in front of me grabbed his dick yelping in pain. He looked like he wanted to kick my ass, that's why I hopped up from in between his thighs and slammed my back up against the wall searching for something to hit him with just in case he tried to harm me. I knew one mark on my face could cause Scarface plenty of money because he didn't allow us to work looking fucked up. He had a stylist who came in every other day to style our hair. He made sure we had facials. He made sure everyone's personal hygiene was up to par. Every week we had a lady that came to wax us. He even had an OBGYN on his payroll that came in and gave us pregnancy test, pap smears, birth control, and just full out exams. This wasn't the average hoe house he was running. This was more like an upscale kind of Brothel. We lived in luxury. We had some of the nicest shit. We had our own rooms and slept on silk sheets and shit. We had a chef that cooked us breakfast, lunch, and dinner. We had a 'house mom' that acted as a mother figure to us. Yeah, to some chicks, this may have been the life, but for me it wasn't. Some girls were here because they lived better here than they did on the streets. Then there were the girls like me who were here by force. Like me, they too got caught up in something involving themselves directly or indirectly and had to clear a tab because it meant life or death for them or a loved one.

I hated this shit so much that unless I had a drink first, it was hard for me to get the job done. I had been with many different men at this point that I just stopped counting after the first five. The clients were weird as hell too and each one of them had a different kind of fetish. Some of them wanted to pay just for me to listen to them talk about their problems at home with their wives. Some wanted a simple oil massage while they lay butt ass naked. Then, you had the real perverts who wanted to watch me touching on myself. The ones that actually did want some sex from me really freaked me out and those were some of the roughest times for me. Although I had lost my virginity at fifteen, this shit here wasn't the same. I felt violated in the worst way. Most of the time I just closed my eyes and lived in an outer body experience while working because if I didn't, I would've lost my soul in this bitch months ago. I had one rule and one rule only, I would lick some balls here and there, but I wasn't sucking no dick. I didn't let nobody touch me without a condom, and I didn't play that kissing all over me type of shit either because to me, that's just way too personal. This particular bastard still squirming like a fucking fish had tried me way too many times. He agreed to getting his droopy ass balls played with and sucked on a little bit but after the third attempt of him trying to shove his tiny dick in my mouth, I bit his punk ass. "This bitch bit me! She bit me!" He yelled out again right before hopping up holding himself with one hand and using the other hand to bring his open hand across my face.

I tried to move out the way, but it was too late. The stinging that I felt brought on a taste of blood in my mouth right along with it. I wasn't gon' sit back and just let him beat on me though. Quickly rebounding, I hopped across the full-size bed and grabbed both of the big boots he had on sending them both flying to his head with all of my strength.

Bloop!

Bloop!

Were the sound of the boots connecting. His fat ass looked like a damn fool trying to leap over the bed like I was really about to let him catch me. Just as I was looking for something else, the door swung open and Scarface was in the room; literally, his entire presence was all in the atmosphere whenever he showed up. The hairs on the back of my neck stood up.

"What the fuck goin' on in here?" He growled looking unpleased and aggravated. He had on one of his expensive suits per usual. He put me in the mind of 'Ghost' from Power. Not even about his looks, but because his presence demanded respect.

"This crazy bitch bit my dick! I want my mu'fuckin' bread back yo! Fuck this bitch!" He barked while grabbing his shit trying to hurriedly put everything back on. I was out of breath and my small perky breast were moving right along with my chest. I bent down and grabbed my robe wrapping it around my tight body before tying it around my waist. Scarface gave me a fucked-up look, but I could tell he wasn't too happy about seeing a handprint in my face. Without another word, he up the burner from his waist and cocked it. Walking to dude, he grabbed him and in one swift motion had the barrel of the gun in his mouth. All that shit this big nigga was popping before was dead. That tough guy shit a few minutes ago was replaced with fear.

"What you say you wanted back nigga? You think you gettin' paid after puttin' yo mu'fuckin' hands on my property?" His voice was low and cold. That one vein that always popped out when he was mad was visible now. The dude was trying to talk but he couldn't because the gun had his words muffled. Scarface shoved it deeper causing him to gag. "What was that nigga?" He taunted him putting his ear a little closer. "Oh, you can't talk wit' my hoe in yo mouth huh? If I didn't want to fuck this room up, I'd blow yo brains out right now. Rule number three, no hittin' on the bitches. Look what you did. Now you costing me money and problems. Get the fuck on. Yo membership is revoked.... fo' life mu'fucka."

Right on cue, Big Bird and a few more of the security niggas that he had post up around here came inside to get dude. Big Bird gave Scarface a look and I knew what it meant because I had seen it before. This nigga wasn't about to make it back home to his family. This whole little incident was about to cost him his life. I shook my head and swallowed hard. It was never my intention for anybody to die, but Scarface didn't give a fuck about that. I knew I was in trouble the minute he closed the door and sat on the chair with his gun in his lap. He massaged his temples trying to gather his words. He could try to hide it all he wanted, but he had a soft spot for me. When the other girls did shit, he would whoop their ass. Funny, he didn't want anyone else hitting us because he was the only one allowed to and it was never the face. It was always body shots and even those could be covered with makeup.

"Why you bite him?" He asked looking me directly in the eyes.

"He wanted me to suck his dick. I don't suck no dick. You know that." Every time I was around him, on the inside I was scared as hell, but on the outside, I had mastered trying not to show fear.

Anger flickered in his eyes when he hopped up. In a split second his hand was wrapped around my neck and my feet were being lift from the plush carpet. "You do what the fuck I say you gon' do. If a client wants his dick sucked, what the fuck makes you think you exempt? I'm gettin' real tired of yo' lil stunts Mani. You costing me money over silly shit. You know the job. If you continue to disobey me, you know you'll be punished." He warned letting me go. I fell to the floor holding my neck while crying. He always tried to control me like a father talking to his child. However, I'm sure if he had a daughter, he wouldn't be pleased about somebody tricking her out to pay off a tab.

"This isn't my fuckin' job! Nigga, no matter how much you try to dress this shit up, it's a professional hoe house and you're fuckin' sick!" He was so sick in the head, he took any insult I threw at him as a compliment but at the same time, he would never let me get away with back talking to him. "When am I done paying you off? Where the fuck is my daddy?! What did y'all do to him because he would've come for me by now! Where is he?!" I was practically yelling causing a scene and he hated scenes. He aggressively lifted me up by one arm and forced me out of the room and down the long hall lined up of other closed-door rooms that some of the other girls were working out of. I originally thought he was taking me upstairs to my main room, but when I realized he was taking me downstairs to the basement, I panicked. "Wait! No! Please! Not the basement Scarface! I won't do it again!" I begged as I kicked and screamed and fought trying not to be tossed down there like a piece of trash. It was dark in the basement. The only light was from a tiny lamp. The concrete floor was hard. If I wanted to piss, I had to do it in the bucket siting on the floor in the far-right corner. It was literally nothing in there and one of the worse places to be.

Just like I knew he would, he tossed me like a rag doll. I hit my elbow hard on the concrete causing it to sting. Because that only little lamp was on, I could see him glaring down at me. One look at him, how professional he dressed, and the way he carried himself you'd never think that he was a monster that had all of this shit going on. I'd found out from the other girls that not only is he a Drug Lord, this nigga runs at least five other Brothels spread out across South Florida and Georgia. Just fucking sick… a sick ass millionaire. "I like you Mani, I really do. You one of my favorites and I wish that shit didn't have to be like this." He paused for a brief second and then continued. "If I keep letting you get away with shit, they gon' expect the same thing and I can't have that."

I was just tired of all of this shit. This isn't the way a seventeen-year-old girl should've been living. I should've been out enjoying life with my friends and turning up for my senior year. I often wondered if anyone besides my daddy was looking for me or had even known that I'd went missing. Maybe the school just thought I dropped out or my daddy packed me up and moved me away after the incident. I'm sure everyone at school had been talking about it months ago when it happened. I wiped a tear from my eye. "When can I go home?"

"When you can pay off the remaining hundred thousand dollars you can go."

A hundred thousand dollars? I thought to myself. "You mean to tell me you have all this money and you're crying about that amount? He can pay you that with his eyes closed! Why don't you just ask him for it? You didn't have to do all of this!"

He chuckled. "Trust me, it's way more than that. That's the price with the discount because I actually have a soft spot for you Mani. Besides that, it's the principal. He should've made sure he was here to keep his eyes on his ship instead of runnin' in and out of town. If you can't pay attention to your crew, you can't pay attention to all of the shit the eyes aren't supposed to see. He's a decent dude. I actually like the nigga. He just got involved with the wrong people. That stash warehouse that got robbed of all that dope was my shit, now that's on his hands. That's what happens when you get caught up with the wrong niggas."

Since my daddy never had me in his business, I didn't know what the fuck he was even talking about right now. I knew it was something, but I never knew the details. I couldn't take the torture of the unknown. The more he spoke, the more my heart broke. "Just tell me... is he alive?" In my heart, I felt like maybe he wasn't alive because if he was, there's no way I would've been here this long. He would've risked his life to try to find me and just the mere thought had me wanting to vomit.

Scarface didn't look like he had an ounce of empathy for me. Deciding not to entertain anymore of this conversation, he replied, "you can stay in here for the night and think about what you did." He turned out and left me right here. From the outside, I could hear him locking me in here and wanted to scream again although I knew it was no purpose in doing so. Just like a little baby, I balled up in fetal position trying to remain strong cause being weak wasn't gonna get me nowhere.

Chapter Three
Tray 'Snow' Harris

We still hustle til' the sun come up, crack a 40 when the sun go down, it's a cold winter, y'all niggas better bundle up, An' I bet it be a hotter summer, grab an onion. Yes, the ROC gets down, you hot now, listen upDon't you know the cops whole purpose is to lock us down? An' throw away the key, but without this drug shit, your kids ain't got no way to eat. Even though what we do is wrong!

What We Do by Beanie Sigel, Freeway, and Jay-Z blast through the DJ speakers on the corner of the block. This had to be one of the coldest nights of the winter and niggas was out on the streets poppin' bottles, rollin' joints, and breakin' bread. The kids ran around with big coats on, the crack heads were doing what they did. The hoes were freezing with their little ass shorts on trying to bag a baller. Then you had us, the niggas that was really gettin' money.

Standing on the outside of 'Da Towers', I could see what the naked eye couldn't see. The sixteen-floor building was home to a lot of low-class families in the hood, so although running an operation, it was my job to make sure shit went smooth around here. It wasn't the best area being dead smack in the middle of lil Haiti, which is one of Miami's toughest areas, but the money was good.

We didn't fuck with no punk ass OPP's over here. The Boonk Gang ran this side of the hood and any other rival gang knew not to come over here lurking. As much as I didn't want to be here day in and day out, this shit had to be ran under the right supervision, especially for the money that was coming in. On the roof, I had the snipers who were in charge of watching everything coming in and out. They had to keep their eyes on the block boys at all times by being the eyes they didn't have from the blindside, cause on gang, I wasn't letting none of my lil folks get robbed or set up.

We didn't beef with other niggas unless we had to. We didn't do no senseless killings, and we ain't drawing dumb ass attention to ourselves that we didn't need. If we had to up on a nigga, it was for a good reason. We were moving so much dope that we were bringing in at least 300k a day and no matter how many dirty ass police my ol' boy had on the payroll, I still didn't need that kind of heat around here. The majority of the money was being washed up through local laundry mats, corner stores, and daycare centers. At only twenty-one years old, I knew the power I held. Niggas knew the power my family held, and the way I ran this operation, I could do this shit with my eyes closed. By the time I was thirteen, my ol' boy connected me with some bad ass Russians that he had business with and them mu'fuckas taught me everything from how to shoot to how to fight. By the time I was fifteen, I knew the family business and the rules that came with it very well. Under no circumstances did I ever tell the family business. That was just a code we weren't supposed to break. By the time I was sixteen, I was graduating high school early. At nineteen, I was graduating from community college with a degree in business. As soon as I walked that stage, my ol' boy turned over 'Da Towers' operation to me while he handled his other shit.

The females around here treated me like God. I had females twice my age that did anything for me. I didn't go hungry because they cooked for a nigga. They did anything I asked them to and I had some gangsta bitches that would ride for me if I needed them to. I made sure I looked out for the single mama's over here. If they were short on rent, I took care of that. If they needed a little extra cash because them kids needed school clothes, Christmas or birthday gifts, I handled that; under one condition, they had to be doin' something with themselves. If a bitch was just layin' on her back fuckin' niggas for free, I wasn't fuckin' with that. However, it was some real good females around here that was trying to make it out here, they just ran into some hard times. I could respect that.

"Yo Snow!" My nigga Reece called my name over the loud music walking up to me. This was the only nigga in the hood that had a Chinchilla on. Clapping me up, he held on tight to the duffle bag that he was holding. "I heard the streets hungry nigga."

"Well it's dinner time." I replied with my eyes bouncing around one last time making sure everybody was still in place. I motioned for him to come on and unlocked the doors on my matte black G-Wagon. "You got that?"

Reece was my right-hand man and handled all of my gun needs. He got the product, I distributed. Opening the duffle bag, he showed me the Glocks he had along with all of the extended clips. I picked up one and examined it. When I was satisfied, I pulled out a wad of blue faces and passed them to him in exchange for the duffle bag. Reece took the money and sat the bag on my lap just as a commotion broke out. He shook his head, "here go the bullshit."

With my brows furrowed, I hopped out and calmly bumped through the rowdy crowd only to see two bitches named Bird and True going blow for blow. Everybody stepped out of my way when they saw me coming. "Ain't shit to see here! Get the fuck on!" I growled as they scattered like roaches. Reece grabbed Bird and I grabbed True. They were both fine as fuck and I considered them to be the prettiest females in Da Towers, so I didn't even know why they were out here like some chicken head hoes but this wasn't the time or the place.

"Bitch!" True spat still trying to get to Bird. "You fucked my nigga? Tell me you did it so I can drop kick yo ass again!" She screamed to the top of her lungs trying to break my grip. This was the shit I was talking about. I didn't need these kinds of problems and every time it was black folks and liquor involved it was a fuckin' problem.

"Bitch I'll fuck, suck, ride, and whatever the fuck else he wants me to do if he gon' keep cutting that check, fuck ass hoe!"

I could tell that shit hurt True by the way she paused. What I didn't expect was for her to burst out crying and dig her face in my chest for comfort. I wasn't on this kind of shit and I wasn't no emotional ass nigga. Bird was on some real bird shit for that one though. Reece being the nigga he was always had some slick shit to say. He gave Bird a side way look that made her shut the fuck up. "Bitch you got more miles on that pussy than the metro rail." He told her but she didn't give a fuck, which let me know she was one of those females that would do anything for money, and she was down for the get down. I knew what was coming next. "Let me holla at you on some business shit." Reece told her. Before she could say anything, he walked her way and disappeared through the crowd.

I walked True to the elevator and pushed the button to take her up. Her pretty brown face was puffy and red from crying. When she looked up at me, she looked like a baby doll with those big round eyes. I didn't know why she was still fucking with that lame, but I didn't get in bitches business. "You gonna walk me up, Snow?"

I shook my head. "Nah shorty. You too pretty to be out here goin' out bad fightin' bout a nigga. I just thought you should know that." I let her know. When the elevator doors opened up, she stood there like she was waiting on me to say something else, but I needed to go and find Reece. I didn't have time to pacifier no bitch that didn't belong to me. The minute I did, they would be expecting something else. You give a bitch some dick, then they want yo' heart next and I wasn't on that. My mind was tunnel vision when it came to the money and the less distractions the better. I turned to walk off and heard her mumbling to my back.

"You know you ain't shit either Snow! Just a blue-eyed demon!"

She said that out of her mouth, but had I turned around and gave her what she really wanted, she'd be telling a nigga how much she loved me. Pulling out my phone, I called Reece. "Yo!"

"I'm upstairs, come to Bird's apartment." He hung up.

"Fuck." I mumbled turning back around to take the stairs. As soon as I walked in, I knew what time it was. Bird sat on the couch smoking a joint. Her hair wasn't all wild and shit no more. She had it brushed back in a ponytail. Her slanted eyes made her look like a Chinese doll, and her butterscotch skin was glowing. "So wussup man, what the fuck you on? You called that bitch, didn't you?" I quizzed looking at Reece with the straight face. He was my nigga and all, my right-hand man, and I didn't get in his business, but I wasn't fucking with the shit he was on. Not when it came to him dabbling in the other business and shit my ol' boy had goin' on.

Bird sucked her teeth. "I'm grown, I make my own decisions."

I wiped my hand down my face and gave her one fucked up look. "Bird, you like yo teeth?" I asked.

Silence.

"That's what I thought, but you know what? Fuck it... you got it." I growled. "I was just about to save this bitch from making the worst decision of her life but bitches like her had to learn the hard way." I reverted my attention back to Reece. "Aye, you know what? You got it... holla at me tomorrow. I'm 'bout to go shut shit down. It's time." We clapped each other up and as soon as I opened the door to walk out, Chantel was walking in. This bitch was the snake of all snakes and she knew how I felt about her. I wasn't down with the shit her and my ol' boy had going on. I ran dope and guns. I wasn't fucking with running no Brothels and shit. All money wasn't good money and trickin' bitches out wasn't my thing.

"What's good Snow?" She spoke like we were cool, knowing she was one of them two headed people I fed with a long-handled spoon.

"Choke on a dick bitch." I closed the door and walked out, leaving them to do what they do knowing that I'd be seeing Bird again; next time it would just be under totally different circumstances.

After clearing the hood up and making sure everything was back in place, I sat in my truck and turned the heater on while twirling a joint in between my fingers. I did this every night before going home out of habit. Before I got ready to pull off, I got a call from my ol' girl. "Wussup ma?"

"Snow... don't forget you need to be in the building this weekend."

I frowned. "For what?"

She sucked her teeth. "You forgot your own parents' anniversary party? Besides, you haven't been to see us in months. It's the holiday season and I want to see my son. I miss that chocolate face and those crystal blue eyes."

"Damn," I mumbled forgetting all about that. "Aiight ma, you know I wouldn't miss it for the world. Tell Scar I said wussup." I spoke of my ol' boy.

"Will do. Love you son... and be safe out there."

"I will ma, love you too."

She paused. "Snow, I'm serious. Watch yourself. I want to see my son alive and not in a body bag."

"Ma, I got me, believe that."

"Okay... see you this weekend." She ended the call.

On the way to my house in Aventura, I rode in silence and turned the heater up a little more. The streets were lit up with Christmas lights and shit. To sight, it was colorful but in my world the shit was black and white. I hated the holidays because it always reminded me I didn't have a woman to share all this shit with or go home to but as fast as my life was, I wasn't sure when I would ever really be ready for that shit. Plus, you couldn't trust females. Fuck that, I wasn't about to have nobody catching me off my square... not even a human walking around with the sweetest thing in between her thighs that a woman could give a man.

Chapter Four
Chantel

I knew Snow's lil fine ass didn't like me ever since he caught me fucking Scar a few years ago. He didn't trust me, and I couldn't blame him, but what he failed to realize is I was the bitch that brought his daddy millions of dollars a year. Half of the girls in the Brothel, I made it happen for them to be there. Even the ones there on their own free will because they just really didn't have anywhere to go. It was simple. They worked for all of the luxuries they were provided and got us paid at the same time. Paid damn good too. I didn't feel bad about it either because it was nothing to feel bad about. Nobody felt bad for me when my own crack head mama sold me to her pimp at the age of fourteen. Nobody felt bad for me when I started getting tricked out either and contrary to what anybody thought about me, I earned my spot. I lived in the Brothel world for years until I was labeled a madam and able to recruit. I had two jobs. One was getting close to any of the big timers in the dope world and two, was getting girls in the Brothel.

With Mani, I was glad that I held off on her for as long as I did. Originally, my job was to get close to Dru to learn his entire operation. What I didn't expect was to fall in love with him and then have to deal with his spoiled ass daughter. I really tried to like Mani, but the lil bitch didn't like me and I didn't like her. She hated sharing me with Dru and I hated sharing Dru with her. He spent too much money on her in my opinion. She had the life

I wished I had growing up and it burned me with envy. I had to work for everything that I had, and it didn't come easy. She needed to see what life was really like and wake up from that fairytale that she had been living in. I had to admit, I was still kinda bitter about her even being alive. I wanted her ass gone, but I knew I couldn't do it, and neither could any of the other girls at the Brothel because I didn't trust that they would keep their mouths closed. They'd practically suck the skin off of Scar's dick if they thought it would keep them on his good side.

With Mani gone, I felt like Dru and me could have a much better relationship. However, he had been much different since she was gone as well. He had lost his best friend Beano. He lost his daughter, and most of all he lost the army that he did have because he no longer trusted anybody. Dru had managed to shut everyone out, even me. He would do anything to have Mani back, but word on the streets was that Mani was dead and Dru lived with that regret every single day. He swore if it was the last thing he did, he was going to kill Scar. I was positive it would be a cold day in hell before he caught Scar slipping or on his own. I had to be very careful with the way that I moved because I didn't need him to suspect anything. Dru was a decent nigga and all and one of the most thorough out here. I had never known him to do anybody wrong. All he asked was Scar give him time to figure out who hit his warehouse for the dope so he could get it back or kill niggas to pay up. In reality Scar could've done that but deep down inside, I felt like his own bitterness of me falling in love with Dru wouldn't allow him to do that. He would do anything to get up under his skin or belittle him as a man. Scar always wanted mu'fuckas to know that he was in control of everything.

Reverting my mind from Scar and his bullshit, I focused back on the girl Bird. She was okay. The basic hood girl. Pretty as fuck, big hoop earrings, plump ass, tattoos everywhere; the usual. Her chinky eyes stood out to most to me because they were a rare grey color. For the first few seconds, she eyeballed me, and I did the same. "Give us a minute…" I told her as I grabbed Reece by the hand and led him in the hallway. He wore a look on confusion on his face. Reece never really liked small talk. He was about his money so that's all he gave a fuck about. I took amount to admire how sexy he was, but I didn't have time to give him too much admiration because it was cold as hell out here. The powder blue chinchilla he wore only did his looks more justice because he looked like walking money, and not to mention he had a big ass dick, so I heard through the grapevine. His cinnamon skin was perfect, and his dark eyes stared down at me like he wanted to fuck the shit out of me. The big Cuban chunk he wore around his neck was iced out and looked like it costed a grip.

"You gon' keep eye fuckin' a nigga or talk about this money?" He asked me. Like Snow, I knew he didn't really care for me either, and just like I felt about Snow, I didn't give a fuck.

I stepped closer in his space almost body to body with him with my eyes squint. "Reece, if I wanted to fuck you, it wouldn't have to be with my eyes baby. Now what you want me to do with that bitch in there? Is she ready to work? What?"

He chuckled and swiped his goatee. "I won't call you for no bullshit. She's ready and she down. That trick in there don't care about shit but money."

"But does she run her mouth?"

"That aint for me to know. That's for you to know. You need work or not?"

I sucked my teeth and rolled my eyes. "You know what, I got it. Thanks for the referral." I tried to walk off and he roughly grabbed me by the arm stopping me. I gave him one funky ass look and he gave me a cold glare.

Looking me up and down, he licked his lips. "I know you ain't stupid enough to be walkin' around with twenty birds on you right now, but don't play with my money. I'll be here tomorrow, same time. If I have to come lookin' for you, I'ma blow half yo fuckin' face off." He warned. Again, I sucked my teeth and walked away back inside out of the cold. Bird was already dressed and had a bag with her.

"What's your name?" I asked.

"Excuse me? You in my apartment, you should've been introducing yourself the minute you walked in here." I could see what type of chick I was dealing with. A loud-mouth one.

I pulled a wad of money rolled up in a rubber band from my Marc Jacobs purse and tossed it to her. "I really don't have time for the small talk. You ready to work or not?"

Clearing her throat, she eyeballed the money like a kid in the candy store before stuffing it in her own purse. "My name is Bird. So what I gotta do?"

"You gotta suck, fuck… stick your fingers up a nigga's ass if he wants you to."

She shrugged, "aiight for how much?"

"Listen, you'll live a life of luxury, the best chefs, the best living arrangements, and some of the best shit. You get a weekly allowance of $2000 and that's it."

"I can do that." She nonchalantly agreed like it was nothing.

I raised a brow. "Reece wasn't lying huh, so you really will do anything for some bread?"

She looked around. "Just look around sweetie. Anything is better than living here. I guess your boujee ass wouldn't know shit about it."

"We ain't here to talk about me. Ain't a block you been on that I probably ain't been down yet." Another thought came across my mind as I spoke to Bird. She was money hungry so if she was indeed willing to do anything, I had another job for her. "If that's everything you got then come on. Lock up because you won't be back for a while."

She did as she was told with the quickness. When we got to my Bentley, she was amazed. If I didn't know any better, she looked like she wanted to jump on top of the car and fuck it if she could. "This bitch is cold right here!" She squealed in excitement. "This what I'm talking about. Big Bank! I need to be rolling just like this!"

Sensing that this trick was probably gon' work my last nerve, I decided to make the best out of it and really try to like her a little bit. "Before we pull off, I have to cover your eyes." I let her know while pulling out a silk Louis Vuitton scarf from my purse since that's all I had.

Flailing her arms all over the place she got real ghetto. "Aht Aht now why we gotta do all that? Helll nah you ain't covering my eyes lil boujee. I don't give a fuck about none of that."

I shrugged and looked at the time on my Rolex watch. "Well I guess yo broke ass just gotta stay right here in Da Towers since you have a problem with it."

Bird wanted to pop off me and I could tell, if she did... I was ready. There was an awkward moment of silence between us two as we once again stared each other down before we burst out laughing. "On some real shit, I really don't like you right now." I chuckled.

She was still laughing as well but she did snatch the scarf from my hand. "Well, I really don't like yo ass either. I'll just wear the shit if ion have no other choice but that don't mean that I like it."

Rolling off into the crisp night air, I whipped the big body Bentley through the streets while constantly peeking at Bird to make sure she wasn't trying to look. I couldn't show her where she was going. None of the Brothel girls knew the exact location of where they were. "You ever killed anybody before?"

I thought I heard her neck snap when she turned it in my direction as if she could really see me. "Say what?"

"Did I ask something wrong?"

Taking a deep breath, she mumbled, "I don't know what the fuck I done got caught up in," she replied shaking her head. "Tell me more. Wussup? And how much?"

"I don't really want you to kill anybody... I mean, if it comes down to it, I'll tell you when and how but right now, I need you to make this money, stay out of Scar's way while doing it, and get close to this little bitch named Mani."

"Who the fuck is Scar?" She asked with a sneer on her face.

"Your new daddy, but don't worry about him. Did you hear what I said?"

"Bitch you big trippin' cause I only got one daddy and that mu'fucka ain't ever did shit for me. Who is Mani?"

I wasn't about to go back and forth with Bird about Scar because she would learn soon enough. "Oh, trust me, you'll know. She's the prettiest, most entitled bitch up in there. Only difference is you're going by choice so you're on the third floor and get a little more access to freedom in the spot. She lives on the first floor because she has to be watched a little more. She's not there by choice."

"What's yo beef with the girl?"

I wasn't down with Bird probing in my business. It was none of her business what the beef was. "The questions you're asking too many and that's the last thing you should do in there."

"Whatever, I don't really give a fuck, as long as you slide me a little extra to be your spy, I don't mind. You want me to get rid of the bitch I'll do that too, but you gon' have to pay me some real big dough. Like a bag BAG! And when can I leave? Whenever I want out?"

I shook my head at how naïve some of these girls could be. What the fuck would make her think she could leave when she wanted out? "No, if you go by choice you have to stay at least six months."

She didn't say anything else. I drove to the three-story mini mansion and drove right past the guard gate because he knew not to stop me. I had just as much as free access to this place as everyone else. Before getting out, I grabbed my purse and my 9mm. "You can take it off."

"Thank God, a bitches eyeballs were starting to sweat under here," she complained slowly removing the scarf. Her eyes lit up when she saw what we were in front of. As a matter of fact, her mouth didn't stop rambling about how beautiful it was all the way up until we made it to the door where we were let in. Stepping inside, I instructed her to follow me. Scar's right hand man Chico was sitting at the bar cleaning a few guns. Chico was a real cutie, but he looked mean as hell. He always kept himself dressed nice and his curly hair was always braided back. The unibrow was kind of sexy to me but it wasn't a lot of girl's preference. Everyone here knew that Mani referred to him as Big Bird and he hated that shit; and although I didn't fuck with her, I thought the shit was funny too. "Chico, this is Bird, the new girl. Take her to Lorraine for me while I go and talk to Scar."

She spun around rolling her neck with an attitude. "Aht Aht, we just got here and you're leaving me with this nigga?"

"Oh please, you're a big girl," with my head slightly cocked to the side I asked her, "will I be in the room with you while you're fucking?"

Rolling her eyes, she got the picture and then eyeballed the bar. "I need a drink first. Y'all got some Fireball back there?"

"Chico handle that, I have to go," I then squint my eyes at Bird. "Remember what I said."

I slowly walked off knowing that once she had her drink, she would be in good hands with Lorraine, the house mom. She was in charge of making sure everything was A1. Tomorrow, the doctor would come and do a full pussy examination on Bird as well. The heel of my YSL boots stabbed the marble tile with every step that I took until I reached Scar's office where I didn't bother to knock. As a matter of fact, I was the only one allowed to come inside without knocking. The minute I opened the door, I regretted it. Scar sat in his expensive full grain leather desk chair with his phone in his hand. As clear as Swarovski crystals, his wife Michelle had her entire pussy exposed putting on a show for him while he coached her on what to do.

Using one of his hands, he massaged his dick through his pants as he slowly licked his lips. To avoid swallowing a big lump in my throat, I pulled out a joint from my purse, leaned up against the wall, and lit it up slowly puffing on my Lah while he ignored me. Everybody knew how much

Scar loved his wife, including me but if you asked me, she was another naïve one. She wasn't obvious to none of the shit he had going on around him, and if she was, she acted as if she didn't. She was one of the most successful lawyers in the south and married to one of the most ruthless men in the south. He cleared his throat just as she plunged two fingers into her dripping pussy and moaned until she was squirting in the camera. I couldn't lie, she was a bad ass female. On a scale from one to ten, she was a fifteen. Scar had paid for her body and her education. The eyes were natural, and that's where Snow got his pretty blue eyes from. "Keep that thing on ice until I get home baby."

She sucked her teeth and whined. "Whennn Scar? This is ridiculous, why do I have to wait so long every night to get dick from my husband?"

"I'll be there. Let me wrap this up." He hurriedly ended the call and tossed the phone on the desk. "Come here." He ordered me with his fine ass.

Slowly walking over to him, I dropped my purse on the floor, removed my jacket, hiked my long wool pencil skirt up, and started unbuttoning my blouse until I reached the desk. Sitting on it, I slowly spread my thighs. Without another word, Scar tore my thong off, whipped his big, throbbing dick from his pants and plunged it inside of me causing me to gasp while holding on to his shoulders for dear life. Putting a deep arch in my back, I spread my thighs even further and used two of my fingers to apply pressure to my swollen clit. Gently biting down on my shoulder was a way for Scar to not scream out at how good I felt to him as he pounded in and out of me furiously like I didn't even matter. Scar never made love to me, not once. Every time he touched me, he was fucking me, but I was used to it. On the other hand, sex with Dru was nothing like this because he always took his time with me.

"Ahh... shit!" I moaned when he reached my spot. The little beads of sweat trickled down his forehead and his physique body handled the shit out of me. Scar wasn't hardly worried about me as he took any of life frustrations that he had out on me. I didn't care because his juicy dick always got the job done. When I felt like he was about to rupture, I bit down on my bottom lip and rotated my hips into his motions until I felt my walls contracting around his dick. "Fuckkkkk." I bucked my hips while gripping his ass trying to pull him further into me until I felt a ripple in his dick as he bust inside of me. As soon as he finished, it was as if nothing happened. He did what he always did, he walked away into his private bathroom to go and clean himself off.

Hopping off of the desk, I followed him, ignoring the sticky juices in between my thighs. Retrieving a rag from the small linen closet, I ran it up under the warm water and then wiped myself down while watching him do the same. "The new girl is here. She's ready to work."

"Good... good. I'll get up with her before I leave." He nodded his head while fixing himself back up. Deep down inside, I had mad feelings for Scar, and I felt he had some for me too and that's why he never wanted to look at me after fucking me. As if he felt bad about not doing me better than just treating me like one of the hoes.

"Look at me Scar…"

"Don't start this shit…"

"Scar, I'm serious."

He walked out back to his desk and focused on the monitors to see what the girls were up to. "What did you say her name was? She's actually pretty as fuck. I think she'll do good here." He suggested.

"She probably won't stay past six months." I replied with an attitude because I didn't want to talk about Bird right now, plus I really didn't like the way he was looking at her.

"All the volunteers say the same shit and they're still here. I treat my hoes good here. They ain't gon' go nowhere else and live like this. You worry about your job and I'll worry about mine."

I hated showing emotions to this nigga because it was like showing emotion to a brick wall. Popping my perky breast back into my bra, I buttoned my blouse back up and put my jacket back on. "You love me Scar?"

Without looking at me, he replied. "Go home to your husband."

With tears in my eyes, I shook my head. I didn't understand how it was possible for me to even have any type of anything with Scar. He treated me better years ago when I was sold to him but ever since he put me on Dru, he felt a way about me for actually loving the nigga. At the same time, I was his best recruiting money maker and if he didn't know shit else, he knew he could trust that I was going to make him some money. "I need twenty bands to pay the nigga that gave me the girl." I let him know because I wasn't paying out of my money.

He walked over to the safe that held his money and his guns and gave me forty instead. I already knew the other twenty was for my pockets since he had to pay me as well. In two weeks, Bird could make him back double of that because only big ballers were allowed to come through here, and not just anybody. All the people that came through here were VIP clients. Without another word, I picked my purse up off the floor, looked at Scar one last time and then walked out closing the door behind me. Sometimes, you had to just charge shit to the game and now it was time for me to go home and play Hollywood with Dru since I'd been gone way too many hours. I couldn't say that I was right, but I had to do what I had to do.

Chapter Five
Mani

Scar left me in lockdown for two days before letting me out. The entire time I had to place my mind elsewhere. I thought about Zayla a lot, wishing that things would've turned out differently. I thought about my last time being free. My birthday party was lit, and I knew it would've been the talk of the year. I had a damn good dream as well. Zayla, Tricia, and I were on South Beach chasing all the big timers without a care in the world. After we did that, we stopped by 'Fat Daddy's' juicy burgers and ate until we felt like we were about to pop because we were so fucked up. Thinking and dreaming about all of the good shit is what helped me to survive those two days.

When Lorraine came to get me, I was so weak. I could barely adjust my eyes from the dark room back to the bright lights. "Come on Mani, let me get you washed up and stuff baby girl. If you want to stay out of here, you gon' have to follow the rules. Trust me everything will be okay pretty girl." She said while rubbing my back. She had a shot of patron waiting for me because she knew I would need it. "Here, drink this."

Grabbing the shot glass from her, I downed it without so much as frowning at the burn. "I hate Scarface's bitch ass, and I hate these nasty ass, perverted ass niggas that come up in here too."

"I know Mani, but it'll be over soon. Seems like you're always in some kind of trouble because you're rebellious and Scar doesn't like that shit at all."

"Fuck him." I mumbled.

Although Lorraine was only in her forties, she played a major role to all of us around here and she was pretty as ever, although she had a mouth full of gold teeth. She was the only female around here that I'd ever seen Scar have the utmost respect for and he never gave her a hard time. After I showered, she cleaned up my scraped up elbow and knee for me and then sent me to get a massage in the relaxation room after that. I cried the entire time, cause I truly hated this shit, but I must admit, the massage felt damn good. I was hoping I could lay in my bed and get some decent rest today but knowing this place, it was probably clients already lined up.

I sat in front of the vanity in a pretty pink robe while getting my hair and makeup fixed. Since some of my polish on my nails and toes chipped when Scar tossed me in the lockup, so I was also getting a fresh Mani and Pedi at the same time. I had missed breakfast so one of the servers brought me a grilled chicken sandwich with crunchy pickles and a side of fresh fries, in which I devoured because I hadn't eaten shit. Lorraine told me and the security at the room door that she would be right back and when she returned, she came back with some other chick who was wearing the matching robe as me. She was about to get the ultimate pampered treatment. Her butt was huge, and she was super pretty to me, but she came in talking all kinds of shit as she flopped down in the seat.

"Somebody could've warned me about having a doctor playing all up in my pussy. That shit is weird as fuck. I've been going to the same doctor for years and I didn't sign up for a new one. Somebody could've warned me. Did they warn you?"

I wasn't looking at her, I was looking at the mirror in front of me. She snapped her fingers in front of my face. "Hello? Can you hear? Don't tell me you're one of those stuck-up bitches."

Snapping out of my own thoughts blinking a few times, I finally acknowledged her. "Huh... you talking to me?"

"Yeah, I'm talking to you. Your name is Mani ain't it?"

I frowned. "How you know my name?"

"Cause, you the prettiest bitch I've seen in here so far."

"Okay, and what does that have to do with you knowing my name?" I pressed.

She shrugged. "It don't matter." Instead of replying, I focused back on my own mirror hoping that she would stop talking to me. "This isn't a job for you is it?" She pried while the stylist got started on her hair.

"What?"

She sucked her teeth. "What floor are you on Mani?"

"Oh... second."

She nodded her head. "Yeah, I can tell."

"You?" I asked.

"Three."

It figures. I thought to myself. Those third times a charm bitches up there on that third floor really baffled me cause it seemed like they never wanted to leave this place even when their contract was up. Lorraine chuckled because she knew what I was thinking. "Be nice Mani... if you're a good girl, you may get picked in the batch of girls to be of service for the Harris's Anniversary party this weekend."

"The Harris's?" I asked confused.

"Scar and his wife." She replied.

I turned around to look at her for validation. I'm not even sure why she was telling me this, but it had to be for a good reason. I wanted to ask her but before I could, Big Bird was coming to the door and pulled Lorraine out to tell her something. I rolled my eyes so hard looking at him and in return he gave me a hard, cold, mean stare before focusing back on her.

"Why you so uptight girl?"

"You wouldn't even begin to understand. Plus, I'm not feeling too well. I feel like I want to vomit." I explained and then got kind of agitated because I was telling her my business and I didn't even know her name. "What's your name?"

She finally extended her hand to shake mine. "My name is Bird." I shook her hand and gave her a half smile right before she started going off on the stylist. "Aht Aht that flat iron is too hot. You don't see the top of my head smoking like a goddamn chimney?"

The poor girl styling her hair didn't even pay her any mind. I didn't blame her. They were probably just as miserable as me to be here. I seriously doubted people just loved Scar that much to want to work for him. When Lorraine came back, she gave me a look of sympathy and sighed. "Look, there's a big baller downstairs and he asked for the two prettiest girls here. The request was for both of y'all."

"Who is the both of us?" I asked feeling my heart drop to the pit of my stomach. I wasn't prepared for this today. I needed more than one shot of patron. I needed at least three.

"You and newbie over here." She replied referencing Bird.

"Why does he need two of us? And it's other pretty girls here. Why can't she go and do it with someone else?" I had tears in my eyes while speaking because just the thought was making me sick.

"Calm down, it's just a threesome. Either that or he wanna watch us fuck each other or something. It's not that deep." Bird shrugged it off like it was nothing.

"A threesome?!" I gasped. "Lorraine, please make them pick someone else. I've never had a threesome." I panicked more so because I didn't want to do it no shit like that. Lorraine looked at me like she was helpless and I could tell she really felt sorry for me. It was all in her eyes.

"How old are you?" Bird asked sneering at me. "You're acting like a lil ass girl."

"That's because she 'IS' a lil ass girl." Lorraine responded to her in a snappish tone defending me.

Bird's whole demeanor changed. "Oh hell nah, they got you up in this bitch trickin' and…"

She paused. "You know what, never mind. Ion no what you did to have to be here but don't worry about it." She then told Lorraine… "We'll go together."

"But…"

Bird cut me off. "But nothing." She winked her eye. "I got you."

"Lorraine, I need another shot, maybe two." I said practically begging with my eyes. She left and came right back with the entire bottle and an extra shot glass in which she gave to Bird. After taking the two shots, I was feeling a little better as I got prepared. Bird tried to have a conversation with me while we waited. I assumed to try to loosen me up. She wore a pretty black lace lingerie set and my little setup was a white lace, two piece with a thong.

"What did you do to have to be here?" She asked with a raised brow.

I leaned up against the wall staring at the ceiling. "Paying off a debt and they won't let me leave until it's paid off."

"Paying off a debt? Girl for who? I'd say fuck that debt and die trying to get the fuck up out of here cause ain't nobody gon' make me do shit ion wanna do, especially at seventeen. These are some sick mu'fuckas."

I sighed and exhaled. "Yeah, well it ain't that simple." Bird looked like it was something she was trying to hold back from telling me. "What is it?" I quizzed.

She shook her head. "Nothing. Let's just get right before this nigga comes up in here. You probably just need a break. I hope they pick you to help with the festivities cause at least it's a breather from here."

"I guess." I mumbled. There was a knock on the door and a fine ass nigga walked in. When I say fine, I meant FINE! His dark chocolate skin was smooth. His bald head was a smooth as a baby's ass and his physique was perfect. Standing about six feet even, I took one look at him assuming he probably weighed about 230. He didn't wear a bunch of ice. He only wore a simple Patek watch on his wrist. His clothes weren't all flashy either. He wore a black tee and some black Robin jeans held up by a Gucci belt. A black pair of Timbs graced his feet. His cologne tickled my nostrils even from where I was standing.

His demeanor let me know that he was one that wasn't going to say much. He may even had been a little ashamed to be here paying for pussy because I'm sure whoever he was in the streets, no one around suspected that he would be in a high class Brothel living out his fantasies. Silently, he removed all of his shit until he was butt naked until his limp dick rested upon his thigh. "Kiss her." He ordered Bird to come and kiss me. I froze cause I had never kissed a female before and never wanted to. Bird motioned for me to come over to the bed, so I did although I wanted to run up out of here and scream.

When I got close, she pulled me down on the bed with her and straddled me. My heart was pounding so fast wondering what kind of shit she was on. "What the fuck you doing?" I whispered through gritted teeth.

She nuzzled her lips in the side of my neck and then licked there before brushing past my ear. "Trust me, I got you." She spoke so that only I could hear. From over her shoulder, I could see the nigga stroking his dick as it came to life. Bird lightly sucked on my neck and I knew if I wanted this to be over with soon, I needed to at least make it seem as if I was enjoying it so that's what I did while we undressed each other. I was wondering how long he was going to be over there stoking himself before he got tired of watching this little show. I didn't have to do shit to Bird because she took control of everything while also making sure she wasn't taking me to out of my element. I realized that she was only trying to help me and that's why she took charge doing her best to distract him from asking of too much.

Walking over to the bed, he joined us both stopping our show and causing me to freeze up. When he laid on his back, he did the unthinkable and lift his legs into the air. Much to my surprise, he didn't have any pubic hair in sight, and most men had hairy asses and ass cracks but his was smooth. He was looking just like us when we got waxed and shit. I looked to Bird with confusion wondering what the hell he wanted and why he had us staring at his ass crack. Without us even touching him, he had his eyes squeezed shut as if he was enjoying it already. The precum oozed from his dick, which might I add was long as hell. "Suck it." He demanded. Bird tried to go for it but he opened his eyes and stopped her. "Not you… her."

Looking at me with regretful eyes, she motioned for me to do it. I shook my head 'no'. "I don't suck no dick." I sneered.

"For the ten G's I just paid, you betta suck my soul through this mu'fucka." He growled. Bird was looking at me like I had lost my mind as she nudged me to just do it.

She started licking on my neck again until she got to my ear and whispered. "Use a lot of teeth, act like you don't know what you're doing."

He patiently waited for me too, and I was freaked the fuck out. I couldn't believe as fine as he was he had his damn legs cocked up like this. I had to position myself on the side of him to be able to reach his dick. Feeling like I wanted to throw up, I swallowed it back down and it burned leaving a nasty after taste. I slowly gripped his dick while staring at Bird. Instead of looking pressed, she was playing with herself and really getting into character as if she was enjoying it. She was a natural when it came to this but not me. All the while she spoke to me with her eyes telling me it was going to be okay and over soon.

Closing my eyes, I forced my lips apart and went down only licking and sucking on the head of his dick. I refused to go any further. I was barely doing shit but he was moaning like he was enjoying it. I was almost ready to just stop when he started fucking my mouth causing me to have more of his manhood in my mouth then I would've like to have. I even forced my teeth in the way a few times but the way he was picking up his pace, I could tell that he was about to nut. "Stick yo finger in my ass ma."

He ordered me. Like a deer caught in the headlights, I completely stopped with his shit still rested in my mouth. My eyes looked at Bird in horror. Wasn't no way I was about to stick my goddamn finger this nigga's dookie chute. He had lost his mind. I didn't give a damn how fine he was.

Before he could catch on to what was going on, Bird rolled her eyes and stuck her finger in his ass instead. She slowly worked it in and out and finger fucking him while he moaned and squealed like a little bitch. When I felt him about to rupture, I abruptly removed myself because I could see me freaking out now if this stranger would've bust all his babies in my mouth to swim around in my damn throat. His body convulsed in a spasm as he shook harder than a stripper on stage. Bird and me both kind of froze up for a minute waiting to see what he was going to do next. I was hoping he was done, but he wanted his money's worth. Little beads of sweat perspired on his forehead and when he stood up, his dick was still hard and ready for another round. "Eat her pussy." He told Bird. I didn't think I could take any more of this shit. I was really trying to stay out of trouble to avoid the basement but this just wasn't working for me. Bird saw the look in my eyes, but again, she spoke to me so vividly with hers. Without speaking, I found myself on the bed and laid on my back spreading my thighs. I tried to think about anything besides what was about to happen right now. Almost positive that this wouldn't be his last request, I sucked it up like a big girl. Bird handled me so gently when she placed her tongue on my silky opening but she barely did anything. Within' a couple of seconds she stopped.

"Oh hell nah! Get up and get out." She ordered me pointing to the door leaving me mad confused about what she was doing.

"The fuck you doin' ma?" The dude asked ready to see yet another show.

Bird ignored him and focused back on me. "I know blood when I taste it. Your period is coming down and I'm not sucking on no bloody pussy. Now go and tell them to send somebody else."

I gasped feeling too embarrassed and hopped up just as quick to grab my shit before running out of there with tears running down my face. Glad that this was happening, but at the same time mortified, I ran out the room, past the security dudes and went to find Lorraine in the powder room. She was overseeing some of the other girls getting dolled up and ready for clients. When she saw me, she excused herself. "What happened?" She frowned. "Did he hurt you?"

I wiped my eyes and refused to let another tear fall because the last thing I wanted was for these bitches to see me weak. "I need a box of tampons."

I could tell what she was thinking. Why would I be crying about a box of tampons?

She rushed away and came back with a new box of Tampax Pearls. "Thanks." I mumbled waiting for one of Scar's big, stupid looking ass, fake security to escort me to my room, because I knew somebody would. I had to go into one of the two restrooms on my floor first. Sucking my teeth, I sat on the toilet and peed expecting to see some blood when I wiped myself. A crease formed in between my eyebrows realizing that there was none. Now that I thought about it, I still had another week before it was time for me to get a cycle. I realized exactly what happened now. Bird did what she had to do to save me of anymore humiliation when it came to that freaky ass man. She knew I was uncomfortable and did what she had to do to get me out of there. As soon as I saw her again, I would thank her because right now I was truly grateful for her.

I didn't want to do shit besides get in the bed and lay down so that's what I did. My room wasn't that big, but it was luxurious and comfortable. The silk sheets felt good on my body. When I heard them locking me in from the outside, I gagged and once again had to stop myself from vomiting. The bitches on the third floor could roam freely, but us down here on the second floor got locked in our rooms and they were always watching us. Even if we tried to run away, we didn't even know where the hell we were. I fell into a deep sleep within no time and when I was being awakened, it was because I heard the door being unlocked. In came Scar's bitch ass. He leaned up against the wall and fold both his arms across his chest. "Wake up sleeping beauty." I cringed at the sound of his voice. Without sitting up in the bed, I answered still under the covers wondering what he wanted. "It's dinner time."

I looked at the clock on the wall, he was right. This would be the time that the chefs would be coming by bringing us our gourmet meal. However, every Sunday he made us all eat together as if we were one, big, happy family and we weren't. The only happy bitches up in here was the willing prostitutes upstairs. "I'm not hungry."

"What you did today, I'm proud of you. See what happens when you behave? You can sleep in your own bed. The sooner you work this debt off, the sooner you can go."

"Yeah, okay." I really didn't get him. We weren't friends and I didn't want to talk to him. I'm not sure why he even thought I would want to be cordial with him. In my eyes, he was a fucking monster.

Ignoring my snide remarks, he continued. "I heard you had a situation. What happened?"

"I'm straight. I bled a little bit but it was nothing." I lied.

"Was it a period?"

"No." I replied. "And no, I'm not pregnant either."

"I'ma have the doctor check you out tomorrow."

"Anything else?" I asked.

He paused and just stared at me with those dark eyes. "I'm tryna be patient with you Mani, but that slick ass mouth; you better remember who in charge."

I gulped and swallowed hard thinking about being thrown back in the basement. "Okay Scar."

Rubbing his hand across the top of his head, he finished taunting me. "There is another thing. You working at my anniversary party this weekend so be ready." He closed the door and locked me back in before I could say anything else.

It wasn't shit exciting to me about working his anniversary party, which I'm sure was a private party at a private location. I was beyond miserable and just that quick, had made my mind up. If he allowed me to work his bitch ass party, I was definitely going to try to escape. As if he knew what I was thinking, he unlocked the door and peeked around the door causing me to jump. "Whatever you thinkin'. Get that shit out ya head cause it ain't gon' happen." He growled closing the door back. This time, I rolled over and cried.

"I HATE THIS MU'FUCKA! UGHHH!" I yelled to the top of my lungs hoping that when I opened my eyes, I had another good dream.

Chapter Six
Snow

After running around all day trappin', I had to hurry up and shoot home to shower and get dressed for this anniversary party. Not that I wasn't happy for my folks or no shit like that, but I had much rather been making me some more money or post up in Da Towers making sure shit was good, especially since this was the month of December and the month niggas got the greediest. I had some of the most thorough females in the building as my eyes when I wasn't around. They were fucking half them niggas and knew to keep their eyes open. If something didn't look right or they heard anything I should miss, they knew to hit me up on the pager. I didn't give a fuck about who was doing what or what was in style. Sometimes, you had to do shit the old school way and that part I learned from some OG's in the game. I had seven different trap phones, and not one person had those numbers, not even Reece. If they needed me, they had to hit me on the beeper, and I'd call back from one of those numbers.

In my opinion, a lot of niggas got cased up because they were too much into this new technology shit. I had an iPhone for my personals, my ol girl, and a few of my family members and even with that, I always kept my location off and I didn't do none of that social media shit either. The Feds was on there too and you had dumb ass niggas wanting to get on there and splurge. If my personals wanted to talk, it had to be on FaceTime cause the Feds couldn't record FaceTime conversations, although I would never discuss anything out the way on my personal phone, it was the principle of the matter. If I ever had to do dirt, or do a big drop, I never took my iPhone. Wherever my back-up alibi would be just in case some shit popped off, that's where I'd leave my phone. I didn't give a damn if it was a bitch's house. I'd never give them mu'fuckas the satisfaction of pinging my location or pinning me near some towers where I wasn't supposed to be just so they could pin a case on me. Wise beyond my years, I studied this shit. I was also smart enough to know that the end goal of a street nigga should be to raise a family somewhere with my future wife, in a big ass house with a picket fence, while throwing barbecues with my niggas discussing how we escaped this shit.

I pulled up in front of the private mansion rental that they had for the night. The outside was lit up with bright Christmas lights and foreign whips, because of course in this world, if it wasn't foreign, it was borin'. I stepped out in all black wearing Versace down to my shoes. I made sure I had my Glock in the small of my back, my .45 was on my waist, and I left my .9 in the G-Wagon. I had 'The Black Box' from 'A Million Roses' in one hand and in the other hand, I held a small jewelry bag from 'The Ice Box' that held an iced out, full diamond dial Rolex watch with the Jubilee band for my ol' girl. I had one of my connects in Atlanta to have it shipped to me in time for tonight. My ol' girl was my heart, and it wasn't shit I wouldn't do for her.

Scar on the other hand, I loved the ol' boy and all, but we never really had a real father, son relationship. Everything with him was always business. He was more concerned with raising me to be street smart opposed to building a real relationship.

I already knew the shit was about to me more so like a player's ball up in this bitch because that's how Scar rolled. It was only family in the spot when it came to personals. All my ol' girl's brothers were ballers, and they flew in from Houston. All Scar's people were ballers and the ones that weren't from here, flew in from Atlanta. Iced out medallions, rings, watches, teeth, earrings, and etc. is the first thing one would notice. One of the female workers dressed in all black came and took my Moncler coat from me to go and hang it on the coat rack. In the middle of the floor my parents held on to each other dancing like they were still just as in love as the day they met at fourteen years old in the Pork & Bean Projects in Liberty City. Scar sang in her ear with the music as the sounds of Lyfe Jennings *Must Be Nice* played.

Cause even when your hustling days are gone, she'll be by your side still holding on, even when those twenties stop spinning, and all those gold-digging women disappear, She'll still be here. Must be nice

Scar swore he would devote his life to making sure she was taken care of. At fifteen, she got pregnant with me and at eighteen they were married living the Bonnie and Clyde life. He's the one that put her through law school because if anything ever happened to him, he wanted to know that she would be okay and could make her own money. Plus, she worked the cases of all of his people who fell into some trouble with the law. Everything was decorated in back and gold, the servers were walking around with hors d'oeuvres, and the hostesses were walking around with the drinks. I was almost positive that the majority of them came from the Brothel, even if the other naked eyes in here didn't know, I knew better. That's one of the reasons why Scar had security extra tight in this bitch tonight, it was to keep a close eye on them.

All of them were dressed in long, tight-fitted black jeans with black button-down shirts. Around their necks were gold bow ties. From the corner of my eye, I could see my aunt Lorraine walking up on me looking fly as hell with her gold Gala styled dress. She looked exactly like my ol' girl although they had the same mother and different fathers. This was a crazy ass world we lived in cause ironically, my aunt Lorraine's father was also Scar's father, which made them siblings as well. Till this day, people thought that was a crazy ass situation, even me but I was used to it by now. Aunt Lorraine was equally as close to both of them although she did work with Scar behind my ol' girl's back.

"Look at my fly ass nephew looking like a bag of money. Let me check you out Snow, because you know damn well you should've been on the cover of a magazine. Um, Um, Um…" She took a step back being extra dramatic and shit like always. "Boyyy just look at those fucking eyes. You need to have some kids to pass them down to. Hell, I wish I had 'em but unfortunately your grandma was generous enough to lay down with that blonde haired white man when she had Michelle. However, she went back to the hood when she conceived me." She shrugged before she gave me a hug.

"I ain't havin' no kids until I get a wife auntie, fuck that. You look good though." I complimented her as my eyes bounced around looking for the nearest hostess to get a drink.

"I know what you want and it ain't on this floor. You gon' have to go to the bar."

With a light chuckle, I excused myself to go acknowledge my parents. I didn't plan on staying that long. I wanted to show my face, grab a drink, probably smoke one and then bounce. The crowd wasn't old cause I didn't have old parents; the shit was just old for me. The only reason I came is because I would've never heard the end of this shit. Everybody clapped and cheered for them when the song went off and I was right there to cheer them on. I mean, my ol' girl was happy because Scar made sure of it. I knew that if she knew about all of his extra shit, it would hurt and I wasn't tryna see my ol' girl hurt. She knew that aunt Lorraine worked closely with him but at the same time, she didn't know exactly what she did for him and had no reason to question it because in all fairness, she's his sister as well so it was no extra questioning there.

As soon as my ol' girl noticed me walking in their direction, her eyes lit up the whole room. "There goes my baby." She smiled meeting me halfway with Scar right behind her. "Snow man, I missed you so much baby boy. You look good too." She smiled while checking me out and shit. I passed her, her gifts and pulled her in for a hug. I remember I used to sit in her lap, and now I lifted her in my arms so that's just what I did; gave her a big bear hug lifting her feet from the floor before letting her go. "You stayed away too long. You always stay away too long."

"I be workin' ma. You know how it is."

She always studied my eyes. That was her way of seeing if everything was okay with me; but each time, she still came up with nothing. "Ever since you were a little boy, your eyes always told a story Snow; and I never knew what you were thinking. Till this very day, I still don't know, but I'm glad you're always okay."

Scar stepped up and we gave each other a fist pound followed by a one-armed hug. "Don't mind yo mama. She always on some mushy shit. What's good Snow?" He stepped back to check me out. He raised a brow. "I know you do yo thing and all, but the money should never keep you away that long."

I ran my hand across the top of my head over my waves. "I be in my bag Scar. You know how it is." I never really called him daddy because in reality, Scar was still young. Hell they both were, and the shit just didn't feel right. He always allowed me to call him Scar as a little boy so it kind of just stuck.

"I'm the one taught you how to get that bag. Don't ever forget where you came from, son."

"Nah, never that. Never forget the family." I replied directing my attention back to my ol' girl watching her gawk over her watch glad that she loved it.

"Ayeeee! Y'all see what my baby did for me? He got me a bust down!" She yelled aloud trying to put it on. "DJ! Play *Ice Me Out* by Kash Doll!" She demanded. As soon as she did, the song started playing and I chuckled. This was the shit I was talking about. She knew shit she shouldn't have known but she was in her prime. I admired her sparkling blue eyes, her dark chocolate skin, her one a scale from one to ten, definitely a ten body. My ol' girl was everything. In the eyes of family, she was just as hood as everyone else. However, when she got in that courtroom dressed up in them bad ass suits, she was a totally different person. I had the best of both worlds when it came to her. Meanwhile, Scar shook his head but as long as she was smiling, he didn't give a fuck.

He excused us from the crowd and stepped off to the side pulling out a joint. He lit it up, took a puff, and then passed it to me. We observed everything around us looking more like brothers standing side by side opposed to father and son. Exhaling a thick cloud of smoke, his eyes bounced around from each girl holding a drinking tray. I didn't fuck with the way he handled them girls, but at the same time, he ran his business, and I ran mine. He didn't fuck up my operations and I didn't fuck up his. I was smart enough to know that Scar would go to war with anybody, including me if he had to. Would he spare me my life? Most definitely but he would damn sho' try to ruin me, that's why I always kept that third eye on him.

"So wussup Snow? I see business is good."

"Fa'sho." I replied not giving much more than that. Scar knew I handled mine and as long as he got his twenty percent weekly, he was cool. My eyes landed back on my ol' girl. She was in the middle of the floor dancing with aunt Lorraine and the rest of her peoples. "She looks happy."

He nodded his head with a look of lust, maybe even infatuation. When you saw a nigga with that look in his eyes, that meant he would kill a bitch for trying to leave him no matter what he may have done to contribute to the failed relationship. Sometimes, Scar didn't understand the dynamics of shit and saw things his way and his way only. As much as I loved the nigga, if he ever physically hurt her, win or lose, we were going to war because it wasn't a soul walking that put fear in my heart. I would rather be carried by six than ever be treated like a bitch.

I pulled long and hard on the joint. Before releasing the smoke, I held it in my mouth for a few seconds. I slowly let out a clouded ring that disappeared right in front of us.

"Well damn, that was rude as hell." One of the Brothel girls fussed while waving the smoke out of her face. She had managed to walk right into the smoke and was choking off of it. She bent down with one hand on her knee so she could pick up the pile of napkins that she had dropped from her tray. When she stood up, I was face-to-face with Bird. The last time I had seen her, I tried to save her ass, but she did what she wanted to do. "Snow?" She chuckled. "Nigga, what you doing here?"

I blankly stared at her without an expression because although she may not have been in the best position in Da Towers, she ain't have to be here going out bad like this. The fact that she was fuckin' for a buck, I couldn't even look at her the same. "Sup," I dryly spoke without answering her questions. She didn't need to know all of that.

"You got something' for us?" He asked her in his way of letting her know she had a job to do and that's what she needed to do.

She cleared her throat, "My bad..." passing us two glasses of Remy, she walked off to the bar. Bird was stacked, so of course as a man, I was gon' look but I'd never touch her like that. My eyes followed her to the bar where she went to re-up and like a sore thumb standing out from everyone else, I spotted a bad ass shorty sitting on a barstool behind the bar. She was dressed like the rest of them, but I could tell from the look on her face she wasn't trying to be here. Like some kind of weird magnetic imprint on a soul, I couldn't stop staring at ol' girl. Shorty was bad as fuck. Her pretty skin was like brown sugar. Her perfect lips were just the right size and heart shaped. Her hair was dyed blue and was styled with soft curls dropping down the sides of her face that landed on her shoulders with a part in the middle. She wore a simple pair of hooped earrings in her ears and she didn't really need that cause she was gorgeous. The make-up she wore on her face only added to her beauty. What stood out the most though were her eyes. She looked like she was so sad. If you asked me, her body was here but her soul wasn't.

As if she felt somebody staring at her, she scanned the room like she was searching for the culprit before her eyes finally landed on me. Just as quick as she spotted me, she turned her head away. Shorty just looked like she was disgusted with niggas. I knew she had to be one of those that wasn't willingly living that life and I felt my blood about to start boiling. This was one of the reasons a nigga didn't wanna stick around too long. "You see something' you like?" Scar asked me, snapping me from my thoughts.

"Where the bathroom at?" I asked. As soon as he told me where it was, the DJ started playing *Cause I Love You* by Lenny Williams and my ol' girl came over with her arms out motioning for him to come and dance with her.

Girl you know I love you
No matter what you do
And I hope you understand me
Cause every word I say is true
Cause I love you

"Tray Senior come on over here and dance with me, baby!" She addressed him by his government name and pulled him into her arms as she started singing. "Cause I lovveeee you. I neeeeed you."

Scar was a different person when he was around her. He was rough, yet gentle at the same time. I used this opportunity to go find Lorraine and I found on the other side of the dance floor sipping on a Heineken. "Snow!" She cheesed. "I missed you so much. I guess we gotta have a lot more anniversary parties to get you to come around." I didn't have time for the small talk, snatching her away from everybody, I pulled her to the corner. "Boy, what the hell wrong with you grabbing on me like that." She fussed looking at me like I was crazy.

"Shorty with the blue hair behind the bar, what's the story?" I asked without wasting time. That wasn't my thing to be beating around the bush. Her eyes led her to the bar until they landed on who I was inquiring about. She was still sitting in the same place uninterested in working at all.

She shook her head. "Oh, that's the baby of the bunch right there."

"Baby?"

"Yeah," she sighed. "She's seventeen, Snow. She's just in a fucked-up situation. Her story is real sad." She shrugged. "I hate it." I knew aunt Lorraine was a hustler, but at the same time, I wasn't buying this bullshit about her hating it cause why the fuck was she there if she hated it so much?

"That's flaw as hell Lorraine, on gang, and you know that shit cause ain't no way you gon' stay somewhere you hate it at." I took a deep breath feeling myself about to go there. "Man… what's the deal with ol' girl?"

Her entire demeanor changed but she didn't shy away from looking me dead in my eyes. "She's Dru's daughter… that says it all right there. She was kidnapped from her birthday party and forced at the Brothel to pay off a debt."

"Dru?" I furrowed my brows. "Dru from da westside? Chantel's Dru?"

"Yep."

I heard all about the Dru's situation and how his warehouse got ran down on so I knew it was some static there, but I never knew he had a daughter involved. I already knew this shit was about control. Scar could've easily let that man pay up but instead, he chose to humiliate his daughter so she can go back and tell him all about it. The nigga probably didn't know she was alive and even if he did, he wouldn't know where to find her. I heard through the streets that Dru no longer had an army. However, I never listened to another niggas business long enough to hear the part about him having a daughter that went missing. He was a cool nigga too.

Lorraine squint her eyes at me, "I know that look Snow. What are you thinking?"

"I just asked what was up with the girl. I'm straight." I turned my back to walk off.

"Snow!" Lorraine said. I turned back around. "Yes, I do hate it. However, just to clear the air, I'm still there because it's girls like Mani who need me. For a lot of girls in there, I'm the closest thing to a mother figure that they're gonna get. I can't just leave them knowing that they need me. If not for shit else, sometimes just for the sanity."

I knew from the look in her eyes that she meant what she said. Without another word, I walked off. I was more than ready to go and get from around this gook ass shit. Making my way to the bathroom, I ignored all of the bitches staring at me out the corners of their eyes and went to handle my business. After draining my main vein, I washed my hands before cupping them with some water to throw on my face. Closing my eyes, I inhaled and then slowly exhaled to calm myself down. I got anxious whenever I was put in situations that I really didn't want to be in. When I was anxious, my trigger finger got happy. I wanted to grab shorty and be her savior; not even because I thought she was pretty. It was to save the little bit of soul she was trying desperately to hold on to. However, I knew I couldn't do shit about it because this was Scar's territory, and I was out-numbered. On top of that, she wasn't my bitch and simply wasn't worth the risk.

I got myself together and walked out of the bathroom prepared to leave when I ran dead into lil mama. She was standing in the hallway blankly staring at a side door. I was smart enough to know what she was thinking, and that most definitely wasn't a good idea. She was so much in her own thoughts that she didn't notice me staring at her. "Don't do it shorty."

Her shoulders jumped snapping her from her thoughts when her head damn near snapped to see who the stranger was talking to her. I repeated myself again. "Don't do it. You don't know how many mu'fuckas on the other side of that door or around this mansion. Trust me, you won't make it."

Again, she blankly stared probably wondering why I gave a fuck or was even in her business. She didn't say two words to me, and I was done talking too. I adjusted my guns and walked off hoping that she took heed to what I told her. If she took my advice, I would definitely be seeing her again. My mind was already made up about that.

After excusing myself from the party, I sat in the truck and rolled me a joint to smoke on the ride back to Da Towers. Deep in my own thoughts, I couldn't get lil mama out of my head and it took everything for me to not run back up in there and get her. However, I couldn't intervene in Scar's business or fuck with his money because I knew how I'd retaliate if a nigga tried to fuck with mine. I heard a buzz from my pager and checked the number. Pulling out one of my phones, I called the number back already knowing who it was.

"Speak..." I said.

"Snow, I just wanna put my mouth on it."

Usually, I didn't have time to entertain True, but everybody knew she was obsessed with me no matter how many bitches she tried to fight over her on and off again nigga. I didn't know why she fucked with him anyway. That nigga was from the other side. He wasn't even allowed near Da Towers. My dicked jumped thinking about True putting her mouth on it because she always came with that fire head. We had an understanding though. As a matter of fact, any female I had any kind of relations with understood that I was married to my money and the game. I would never focus on a relationship right now so don't expect shit from me because it ain't happening. At the same time, I had to be careful the way I dealt with females as well. I didn't fuck with the clingy types. Just because you give a female some dick doesn't mean you're ready to give them yo' heart. "I'll be there." I replied before hanging up. Glancing at the mansion one more time, I hoped lil mama was okay. Shaking my head, I pulled off to handle True and then get back to the money.

Chapter Seven
Mani

"Where's the bathroom?" I asked Bird. She was enjoying her night, and then you had me who didn't want to do shit at all. I know Scar noticed and would probably try to lock me down when we got back to the Brothel. At this point, I wasn't even concerned with that. I didn't even understand how he was such a monster with such a beautiful wife. Her spirit was so dope. As a matter of fact, everything about her was dope from her looks, to her personality. She was a whole vibe. It was such a shame that she had no clue where we came from and she probably didn't even care. I'm sure Scar led her to believe that we were the hired help. Some of the third-floor girls were, but not me. I was the only one here from the second floor all because Scar wanted eyes on me. I'm sure the only reason he let me roam the party a little bit was because he had all of this security with eyes on us.

The bathroom was literally right next to the bar in a small hallway, but right across from that hallway was an exit door. In just a few seconds, my thoughts drifted on trying to make a run for it. My heart was beating fast as hell, but my brain was smart enough to know that the minute I touched the door, I still wouldn't make it out. However, my feet were practically stuck to the floor. I literally couldn't move.

"Don't do it shorty." A smooth, deep voice boomed from the side of me causing my shoulders to jump in shock. The same dude I caught staring at me earlier was right here in my presence now and I hadn't even known that anyone was standing there. That's how caught up I was. I blanky stared at him trying to force the lump down my throat. Not because I was being a bitch, but because the sight of this beautiful roughneck nearly knocked all of the wind from my body. His chocolate skin was covered in tattoos from his neck, to his arms, down to his hands. The way his crystal blue eyes pierced right through me had me shook. The thick waves in his low-cut hair had the perfect, crispy tape line around his edges. He wore an all-black Versace outfit. His button up collar shirt went perfect with his slacks, in which I could clearly see his dick print. His feet graced a pair of black and gold velvet Versace loafers with the gold Medusa head. A red Arabic full diamond dial Rolex watch shined on his left wrist.

"Don't do it. You don't know how many mu'fuckas are on the other side of that door or around this mansion. Trust me, you won't make it." He informed me before adjusting the visible burner on his waist before walking off. I didn't know what to think but in just those few seconds, I was drawn to him. When he walked off, I felt like my body was pulling trying to follow him. His words nearly scared me because it led me to believe that he may have knew something about me and my situation. How would he know to tell me not to try to run? What the hell did he know? I heard what he had said but fuck it. It was now or never, and whatever happened just happened. I closed my eyes saying a quick prayer asking the Lord to give me strength.

The only thing that kept me from trying to run out of this door was because I had to remember the bigger picture. I wanted to see my daddy again and I needed to do this for him.

Gathering my thoughts, I took a deep breath and then walked in the bathroom to pee and wash my hands. When I came out, Big Bird was waiting for me. "Give me a fucking break." I mumbled rolling my eyes.

"It's time for you to go."

"What do you mean?" I asked.

"You heard what I said. Scar said you and Bird gotta go back. Let's go." He roughly grabbed my arm and led me out of the same door that I had been contemplating running out of. He was being so rough with me that I almost stumbled over my own feet as he dragged me out.

"Wait! Slow the fuck down!" I tried to snatch away. "And don't be grabbing on me like that!"

He gave me a warning look. "You betta calm the fuck down before I knock yo' lil ass out. I would hate to bruise that pretty face of yours." He scolded while trying my hands behind my back before placing the mask over my eyes. My heart was racing and pumping with adrenaline, but I didn't want to cause trouble right now knowing that I wouldn't win. At the same time, he had me fucked up. I was losing my mind and truly sick of his ass.

When he tried to get me to walk again, I refused while cussing his ass out. "You big cock-eyed mu'fucka. You da type of nigga that sit and jack yo' dick all day because you probably don't get no pussy huh? You's a bitch, a fucking do boy and that's probably why you don't have a bitch. Nobody wants the fucking help. Even my lil young ass knows that! I'm gon' shoot you right between the eyeballs if I ever make it out of here bitch!" I spat hating that I was once again involuntarily staring at the back of my eyelids.

I didn't shut up until he left me with no choice. Slamming his big fist in the pit of my stomach, I winced over in pain while trying to catch my breath. It hurt so badly that I didn't know what to do. That punch was followed up with a swift kick to the ribs. That one took me down. Crying out in pain, I whimpered like a baby. Big Bird was smart enough to know not to hit me in the face, however, he and Scar were big on those body shots. "Bet you shut the fuck up now." His voice vibrated in my ear. I couldn't say anything because I still hadn't properly caught my breath and the pain was terrible. He roughly grabbed me by the arm again removing me from the ground. When he reached whatever vehicle he was taking me to, he tossed me inside. I doubled over on the seat and cried.

Within' moments, the engine was roaring, and we were pulling off headed back to the Brothel. My heart was beating hard as hell as my chest heaved in and out. "Where's… where's Bird? I thought she was coming too." I managed to get out.

"In another car." He replied dryly. I could tell he was tight about the way I had spoken to him. His phone rang and when he answered it, it connected to the radio. He must've dropped the phone trying to switch it back over because he started fumbling for something. "Fuck!" He yelled out.

"Chico, what the fuck is going on? I have three more girls lined up and Scar is tied up so who's coming to handle everything?"

What the fuck? I thought to myself. This bitch sounded exactly like Chantel. No! I knew it was Chantel. I knew her damn voice and my heart dropped. I could feel my lips trembling and the warm tears clouding my eyes again. "Chantel?" I asked aloud.

"Chico, who the fuck is that?" She asked with an attitude ignoring me.

He was still fumbling for the phone... with his big ass. "Would you just shut the fuck up! Stop talking and give me a minute." He demanded. We were now swerving a little bit.

"Chantel! Is that you?!" I yelled. "Bitch! You fucking bitch! You're dead! You're supposed to be dead! I heard them kill you! You trifling son of a bitch! You sick, jealous fucking bitch!" I cried out from the pit of my soul. I couldn't believe I mourned over her being killed and she wasn't even really dead. I felt so bad about it. I was so fucked up knowing that my daddy loved her.

"Mani! Shut the fuck up! Damn!" Big Bird barked before back handing me. I felt the blood in my mouth, but I wasn't done. Due to the circumstances, he didn't give a damn about my face. I guess he finally managed to find the phone because I could no longer hear the car speaker. He ended the entire call, which is what he should've done in the first place. He should've ended the call

84

from the dash the minute he dropped his phone, but he didn't and now the cat was out of the bag.

I cried the entire time until the truck came to a halt letting me know we had arrived. He snatched me from the vehicle and led me inside the Brothel. When we made it inside, he finally freed my eyes but not my hands. From a distance, I could hear a set of heels stabbing the marbled towel and when my eyes landed on Chantel rounding the corner, my knees got weak I nearly gagged. Big Bird stopped me from falling down. Out of nowhere, I became extremely hot and felt faint. I couldn't believe this bitch was standing in front of me well and alive. With a blank stare on her face, she walked right up to me and fold her arms across her breast. "I guess the cat is out the bag huh? How are you liking your new life Mani? I guess you ain't as bad as you thought you were. Life was good with your daddy's money and now your spoiled ass finally gets a taste of what this real shit is all about."

I didn't shy away from her eyes. It wasn't no reason to because Chantel didn't scare me at all. I should've known not to fall for that shit. "Bitch you wanted me to think you were dead so I wouldn't tell my daddy that your hoe ass is the one who helped put me in this predicament." I hissed through gritted teeth. "I knew not to trust yo' ho' ass."

She nodded her head. "You're right, but I guess that doesn't matter anymore since he's dead anyway."

I tried to study her eyes to see if she was telling the truth and I couldn't tell. I had so many mixed emotions right now that it was ridiculous. If what she was saying were true then that meant my only little piece faith that helped me survive this shit was now gone and for that, I wanted to cry in the worst way. At the same time, she couldn't be trusted either, so I knew not to take her word for it. Afterall, this bitch was supposed to be dead her damn self. "Fuck you! Fuck you bitch!" I tried to lunge at her, but she took a step back laughing while Big Bird grabbed me. I didn't see shit funny. I hulked up a glob of spit and aimed right for her face. She moved just in time for it to fly right past her face. "I swear to God I'm gon' beat the black off yo ass when I lay hands on you! I fucking swear!" I was so pumped up, I forgot all about the pain in my ribs, or that fact that my damn hands were zipped tied behind my back. If I could get to her, I surely the fuck would.

"All that jumping around you're doing isn't gon' change shit Mani. This is what it is, and this is what it's gone be. You never understood me or my life. Guess what baby girl, you're getting a taste of it right now. Welcome to my world."

"Fuck what you talking about Chantel. There's no fucking way my daddy is dead and you're alive."

She smirked. "Believe it boo."

I slightly cocked my head to the side and squint my eyes. "You know what? I guess it's really not a coincidence that you're still here and he's not because a coward can live a thousand lives, but a soldier only lives once… ol' coward ass bitch." I spat and then looked at Big Bird. "Take me to my fucking room."

I couldn't hear shit else that Chantel was saying because I had managed to block her out as he led me away. He might've been a foul ass nigga, but I could tell that in this moment, he felt sorry for me because it was all over his facial expression. I wished that Lorraine was here but she wasn't so I had nobody to talk to. The only thing I could do is be locked in my room and cry for the rest of the night. To make matters worse, after stripping out of my clothes so I could crawl under my sheets, I discovered that I had a huge blue and purple bruise forming under my rib cage. Wincing in pain, I slid under the sheets until I finally was able to fall asleep. Christmas was right around the corner and it looked like I would only be able to have a happy one in my dreams.

Chapter Eight
Snow

I hadn't been able to shake the visions of shorty from the other night out of my head and every time I tried, my mind kept wondering the same shit. Was she aiight? Did she try to run? Did Scar fuck her up because of it? It wasn't like me to be in one's business, but I needed to know. I had managed to get some information on Dru and from what I heard, the nigga wasn't doing too good. I couldn't say I blamed him. If my daughter was missing, I'd be trying to paint the mu'fuckin' city red. I could understand his frustrations because the streets didn't talk, and he was a one-man army right now. They said he wasn't even the same right now, like on some real depressed shit.

I cruised through the hood after checking the paperwork from the laundromats, the daycare centers, and the corner stores. It was a whole lot of money laundering going on in my world, but I had to do what I had to do because in a few years, I planned on walking away. It was only two ways niggas usually got out of the game and that was between the grave and the jail. It was only a few that were lucky enough to slip through the cracks. I stopped in front of Da Towers and hopped out to holla at Reece. He stood in the front of the building rubbing both of his hands together trying to warm up. I had paid a company to at least come out and put some Christmas lights and shit on the building for the kids. There was a couple more lights going around the bushes and the trees. In another week, I was hosting my annual toy drive around here. I always gave back to my hood because I knew these mother's needed it.

The kids around here loved me. Whenever they managed to catch up with me, it was always 'Snow this' and 'Snow that'. They wanted lunch money or ice cream money. I knew the lifestyle that I lived was wrong but being able to see a smile on those kids faces to brighten up their dark world made my day plenty of days. Reece and I clapped each other up before giving each other a brotherly hug. The rest of the Boonk gang was in position handling up like they were supposed to do. "Cash money... talk to me nigga." Reece said making sure he didn't take his eyes off of everything else in front of him. That's one thing I loved about Reece. He was always gon' be on alert. This the only nigga I knew that would take a bullet for me with no questions asked.

I peeped the black duffle bag thrown behind the bush right next to him and automatically knew his AK-47 was in there close enough for him to get to it if he needed to. "Everything 1k?" I asked making sure it was all good in the hood.

He nodded his head. "Another 300k week, ain't no complaints."

I rubbed both of my hands together. "Good, good. That's what I like to hear."

"Mrs. Junie came down here lookin' for you earlier complaining about it bein' too cold and the kids needing coats and shit. I handled that though. I gave her a grip to go purchase some." I wasn't sure why he gave Mrs. Junie the money knowing she had a gambling problem. I gave him a look of uncertainty about that move right there. "Nah, she knows what it is. You know if she ain't scared of nobody else, she not finna even play on yo top like that. I told her she had until tonight to come back with them coats or else you were gon' be at her door for breakfast in the mornin'. She knew exactly what that shit meant."

"Good, because I would hate to have to fuck Mrs. Junie's wrinkle pussy havin' ass up cause she on her bullshit."

Reece laughed but he knew I was dead ass serious. The ding from the elevator let us know that somebody was getting off. True and one of her home girls stepped off bundled up in oversized jackets and Ugg boots. I hadn't seen her since the other night when she called me over. "Hey Snow." She sang while she boldly stared at me like she was mesmerized. We had a good time, but she knew not to speak my business in front of nobody.

"Wussup." I acknowledged her. They spoke to Reece next and he did the same but just like me, Reece didn't really like to be out there like that.

"We about to go get some conch fritters and pork souse... y'all want us to bring back some for y'all?" She asked.

"Nah, I'm straight. I'm bout to peel off." I let her know. Clapping Reece up again, I walked off and hopped back in my truck. I played *3AM* by King Von and pulled off mumbling to his words. *Man these niggas be bitches, straight ho' flat out he sissy.*

I turned it up a little more and headed to the last place I ever wanted to go, but this shit sat heavy on my heart and it fucked with me because I didn't understand why. I didn't even know shorty. When I pulled up to the Brothel, I was patted down before they let me inside. They didn't just let anybody through here and it was hard as fuck trying to get past security at the gates. They only let me in off the strength of Scar. I headed straight for the bar where a big black nigga named Doon was posted. He was another one of Scar's men. As soon as he noticed me, he clapped me up. "Heard the weather-man said it's a light chance of Snow... what up lil nigga?"

"It's a cold world nigga. You know I stay dressed for the weather." I briefly looked around. "Where Scar?"

Taking a shot of Patron to the head, he frowned at the burning sensation and then responded. "Oh, he stepped out. What you need?"

I got straight to the point. "How much for an hour with Mani?" Ever since Lorraine told me her name, I couldn't forget it.

Doon raised a brow. "You young niggas payin' for pussy now?"

"What I do wit' my dick is my business." I replied going in my pocket to pull out a wad of money held up in a rubber band. I sat it on the counter in front of him. "How much?" I asked again with not so much as even as a smirk. Wasn't shit about this place funny to me.

Picking it up, he removed the rubber band and then thumbed through it. "Oh, so you serious... aiight give me one second. Let me see if shorty free and make sure she don't have no clients coming within the next hour if she is." Picking up an iPad, he scanned through it and then got back to me. "She's free, she got another client in three hours so you are good."

I pulled out another wad of money and sat that on the counter too. "Cancel it then, I need that slot as well."

I could tell he was wondering what was up at this point, but he'd never speak on it. "Snow, come on man, don't be stingy. That nigga is a very loyal paying customer."

I once again pulled out another wad of money and this time I tossed it to him instead of respectfully sitting it on the counter like I'd done the previous two. "Double or nothin' then. I don't give a fuck about that. Matter fact, that should cover the rest of the day. You gon' lead me to shorty or not?"

"Whew." He whistled wiping the back of his hand across his forehead. He pulled out his walkie and radioed another nigga to come and get me. Some other dude that I didn't know came to lead me to Mani. The entire time his bitch ass walked with his chest poked out like he was the man. I wanted to split his shit wide open. Literally bust his shit to the white meat. I couldn't be happier when he finally stopped in front of the door she was behind. He opened the door and led me in.

"Enjoy." He said before walking off.

Taking a deep breath, I opened the door and shorty was leaned up against the wall wearing a silk mahogany robe with the matching two-piece lingerie set underneath it. Her hair was styled in soft curls and pinned on top of her head while a few tresses softly dropped on the sides of her face. Her make-up was flawless, and her perfect shaped lips wore a mahogany color lipstick that matched her attire. As soon as she saw my face, her eyes dropped into tiny slits. "You again?"

Taking a seat in the chair, I just stared at her. I wasn't here to fuck her, and she needed to know that. I wanted to know exactly what the fuck was going on. "Sit down shorty." I nodded my head toward the bed.

She sucked her teeth and slowly walked over to the bed. I could tell she was in the mindset of being submissive just to get it over with. Flopping down on the bed, she crossed one leg over the other and then pointed directly at me using her pointer finger. "Listen, to avoid you getting mad or getting me in trouble with the Boss, I'll tell you right now. I don't suck no dick and I don't stick my fingers in nobody's dookie chute."

Shorty was on some wild shit but the last thing I wanted to talk about was another niggas asshole. I slowly leaned up until both of my elbows were rested on my knees. Crossing my hands in front of me, I needed her to read my body language. "Good, because I'm not interested in talkin' bout no shit like that." She sat on the bed unafraid to give me direct eye contact. I didn't know her exact age as of yet, but what I did know is if shorty walked in here a little girl before, she was definitely a woman now.

"You'd be surprised of the shit people come up in here requesting and from the naked eye, they don't look like they're interested in some shit like that either." She huffed. "Listen, I'm not trying to be rude but are you going to give me the demands of what you'd like me to do to pleasure you?" She boldly asked.

"That's what I'm doin' ma. I'm talkin' to you. That's what I'm here to do."

A look of relief wore on her face. "Oh, you're one of those kind… thank God. Well, you talk, and I'll listen. That's usually how this works."

"No, I'll ask you the questions and you'll answer."

"Nothing personal." She informed.

"Get comfortable cause this is all personal with me Mani."

Her eyes widened. "How do you know my name? Lord, don't tell me you're one of the stalking niggas. The only people that know our real names in here are the people who work here. My name is Bella to the clients, not Mani." She sneered.

"Is Bella on yo birth certificate?" I asked.

"No… but neither is shorty or ma and you've called me both."

"You got a slick mouth." I told her but it gave me some sense of hope to know that she was still holding on to herself.

She shrugged her shoulders. "Yeah… well."

"How old are you?"

Refusing to answer, she defiantly shook her head. "Un Un how old are you? I don't give my age."

"I'm twenty-one ma, and I'm not one of the fuck ass clients that come in here payin' for pussy either. I told you, I'm not on none of that shit. I simply want to know what's up wit'chu. I saw the look in yo' eyes that night. I know what's goin' on here. I know exactly who ya pops is." I said knowing that should get a reaction out of her and it did. She all of a sudden looked hopeful.

"You know my daddy? Is he alive? Have you seen him?" She bombarded me with questions. She was so excited to hear that I knew her pops, she tried to hop of off the bed and stand up, but she quickly sat back down wincing in pain. "Ouch." She mumbled.

Realizing she was in pain, I stood up from the chair and sat on the edge of the bed. She scooted a few inches away from me. "I'm not gon' hurt you shorty. I told you what it is. Now, what happened to you?" I peeped her holding under her rib cage.

"Nothing, it's nothin'." She hissed. "Just keep talking. So, what about my daddy? I need to know if he's okay and if so if he's looking for me."

I couldn't focus on her words, because I was too busy focusing on her trying to ignore her pain and it pissed me off. Finally, I said fuck it and stood up walking to her until I was standing over her. "Let me see." I ordered.

Mani looked up into my eyes, as if she was second guessing showing me. I wiped my hand over my waves and took a deep breath. "Look shorty, I know this is a lot to ask, but I need you to trust me… can you do that for me? Cause believe me when I say I'm as solid as they come, and I wouldn't waste my time comin' to a mu'fuckin' place I despise just to come see wussup wit'chu. I just paid a grip to clear yo schedule for the rest of the day."

    She cleared her throat and loosened up a bit. "You... you what? Why would you do that? Why would you spend all of that to take up my day?"

    This shit was crazy. I didn't even know her and from the first time I laid eyes on her, I wanted to be her protector. "I'm gon' sit down next to you. Is that aiight?"

    She nodded her head giving me the approval before I sat down. This time, she was a little more relaxed. "You just willingly spend that much money on people?" She asked.

    Looking her dead in her beautiful eyes, I told her the truth. "To my hood, yeah, I give back, spend money, and do shit for the people all the time, but on a female? Nah, because you give a mu'fucka too much too soon they'll value yo' hand instead of yo' heart. It ain't like that wit'chu though, shorty. Believe me when I say I'm on yo' ass. Now please... let me see."

    I could tell the pattern in her breathing changed. She slowly removed the silk robe and let it form a puddle around her waist. "I got in trouble for contemplating running away that night you saw me, and you were right; I should've listened. I insulted Big Bird after that, and he punched me in the stomach right before kicking me in the ribcage." She admitted. Using my finger, I lightly traced the black and blue bruise that had formed, and it looked painful. I didn't want to make her nervous, so I had to refrain from showing how I really felt about it.

"Big Bird?" I asked with furrowed brows.

Pulling her robe back up, she replied. "Well, I call him that, but his name is Chico."

With a simple nod of the head, I shook the thoughts of putting a bullet through his skull out of my mind. One thing I didn't do was beat on a female. I might jack a bitch up if I had to, but I wasn't about to be beating on one. To me, that was some hoe ass shit. "I'm gon' ask you this again. How old are you?" I knew that was probably against the rules for them to even be telling people their real age, but I didn't give a fuck about none of that and I hoped she didn't look at me as a client.

She dropped her head before admitting her age, "I'm seventeen."

"And how long have you been here?"

She shrugged. "I don't even know. I lost track of everything." She sadly admitted. "I don't even think about it no more. Is my daddy dead?"

Using my forefinger, I lift her head back up forcing her to look at me. "Keep ya head up ma. Don't do that."

"Your eyes… they're mesmerizing."

"Thank you…" I responded getting back to the point. "I need to know who to holla at to get you out of here." I already knew, but I just needed to see how much she knew.

That caused her to frown and scratch her head. "Why do you keep going around the daddy questions?"

"I don't want to touch on that... to my knowledge he's alive. That's all I know." I didn't want to speak on him too much, but I just needed her to trust me.

"I'm sorry, but why are you here again?"

"I want to help you get out of here and I need to know what you know."

"I know that there's a debt that has to be paid and until it is, I'll be a prisoner here and my body will continue to be a temple for any sick ass man that comes in here."

"Oh, I see." I replied dryly while wondering if Scar was back yet.

"Why do you want to help me? Are you gon' buy me from them so I can then work for you? What is it? Cause you can't possibly be interested in me in any other way. Like, I don't have shit, not even my own identity right now."

"I don't give a fuck about what you have. If I'm in yo' corner, I'ma fuck wit'chu broke, paid, or hurting. Hard times don't last, solid mu'fuckas do. I'm not askin' shit of you and don't expect shit from you. Don't knock a thug for havin' a heart ma."

Mani got extremely quiet and deep in her own thought. She blankly stared at the wall in front of her. I didn't push the issue. I gave her a few minutes to gather her thoughts. Finally, she looked back at me. "What's your name? All of this time and you haven't even told me your name."

"Snow... my name is Snow." I was almost positive that she'd never heard of me and couldn't out the connection between Scar and I together right now. The only reason I didn't tell her about us is because I knew she wouldn't trust me or would shy away from me.

She chuckled a little with a raised brow. "Snow? That's interesting. I'm sure that's not your real name, so why do they call you Snow?"

"The eyes… and my jewelry is icy."

"I would be cocky as hell if I had those eyes."

"It's a gift and a curse." I admitted. I got little more in her business and intensively listened to everything without any interruptions. I didn't tell her much about myself, but I was glad to be able to open her up a little. She was a sacrificial lamb in this game, and it was fucked up. I couldn't even say I was surprised when she told me about Chantel, however, I was smart enough to know that now that Chantel knew the cat was out the bag, that could bring more harm to Mani. Chantel was a cold bitch and would do whatever she had to do to keep Mani silent or miserable. When it was time to go, I simply asked her for a hug. To my surprise, she didn't hug me, but she allowed me to hug her.

"Will you be back to see me Snow? This is the best time and conversation that I've had since I been here. I could literally talk to you all day."

I gave her a reassuring smile. "I'll be back…. trust me."

"You never told me how you know my name."

"If you've learned anything about me from this conversation then you should know I did a little research before comin' here. I'll see you soon, real soon shorty." I let her know before knocking on the door to be let out. I could feel her eyes burning a hole through my back. Our connection was strong, real strong to the point where I felt that she didn't want me to leave her. Just the same as I really didn't want to go.

Chapter Nine
Snow

I was led to Scar's office and the door was locked. I knocked twice before Chantel was coming to the door adjusting the skirt that she was wearing. "Hey Snow." She spoke finding her way out. I didn't even speak back. I'm not sure why the bitch kept speaking to me. I wish I could knock her mu'fuckin teeth out of her mouth. Brushing past her, I walked in. Scar was sitting on the desk counting some money that he then went and walked to the safe before locking it up.

"Sup son?" He lit a joint and took a pull. He offered me a hit and I declined. "Heard you paid some big bucks for a good time. Finally comin' up out that lil shell I see."

"I'm my own man... been my own man."

"I know." He replied proudly. "I made sure of that."

Nigga was always on some bold shit. "I need to holla at you about somethin'."

Locking up his desk drawers and stuff, he grabbed his keys and walked toward the door. "Cool, but yo mama waiting on me to come home and put the Christmas tree up so you gon' have to follow me there. She'll be glad to see you anyway. Nigga, you know you the golden child."

It didn't make no sense to go back and forth with him. I didn't give a fuck if he wanted me to follow him to Jupiter right now, we were about to have this conversation. "Aiight." I followed behind him until we made it outside. When we arrived at his estates, we walked to the door together. The outside of the house as well as the yard and the driveway were done by professionals who my ol' girl paid to come out and make everything look like Christmas on the North Pole. She did this every year since it was her favorite time of the year.

"Ma!" I called her name when we made it inside. She had a huge tree still tied up laid out in the middle of the living room. She rounded the corner wearing a pair of black tights with a simple cotton shirt. A pair of Fendi slides were on her feet and she had a cup of tea in her hand that she was sipping on.

"Snow man…" She cooed. "Hey baby. You must miss me because I've seen you twice in one week. I usually see you twice every six months. Come give yo' mama a hug."

"It ain't like that ma… don't do me like that." I pulled her into a big bear hug making sure not to cause her to spill her tea.

"Um hmm." She chuckled and then focused on Scar. "Hey baby." She kissed his lips and then frowned. "Why the fuck do you smell like a female? Where the fuck you been?" She quizzed giving him the side eye.

"Come on, Michelle. Don't start that shit. I don't smell like no fuckin' female. Only female I smell like is you."

She gave him that side way look. "Nigga, are you crazy? So, you telling me I don't know what the fuck I smell like?"

"Don't start." He warned.

I knew who she was smelling was probably his side bitch Chantel's trifling ass. I minded my business though.

"Yeah okay, let me find out you're on some bullshit. I'm leaving your ass, and everything is going with me. When I say everything, I mean just that." She snarled rolling her eyes. She then eyeballed the tree. "It's ready for you to put up." She told him. "I'm going back to my office to work on these cases."

Scar stared at her backside up until she disappeared before he addressed me. "Come on, come to my office." He led the way because he didn't want to talk out in the open where she could possibly hear. "So wussup Snow? Everything aiight with the business? This is twice in one week that I've seen you."

I got straight to the point. "The girl Mani, how much is her debt?"

"Why?" He asked giving me that suspect look.

"I want to buy her from you. That ain't no place for that girl man."

"She ain't for sale."

"Well, if it's bout a debt then ion see what the fuck the problem is. You get paid and I take her off yo' hands." He twirled a cigar in between his fingers not breaking his glare from me. Father or not, he didn't intimidate me. "I ain't no bitch Scar. All that intimidation shit don't work for me."

"I'm not tryna intimidate you. Why the fuck would I need to do that? You're my son. I'm just tryin' to figure out why the fuck you're so interested in her all of a sudden."

I clenched my jaws feeling myself getting agitated. "How much?"

"Ain't enough money you can give me to make me give her up. That lil bitch puts a spell on niggas. She's rude, she refuses to suck dick, but she's beautiful. Niggas pay her to watch her sleep and all kind of weird shit like that. No matter how much trouble she causes me, they still keep coming back requesting her. She makes me too much money to just let her leave now."

"So you plan on keepin' the girl hostage the rest of her life? Why the fuck didn't you just let Dru pay you Scar? What the fuck really goin' on?"

"Aye... yo business is yo business and mine is mine. It's been like that for a long time, so let's keep it that way Snow. Foreal, man to man. She's not goin' nowhere. Nigga you act like you got bit by a love bug." He said trying to fish for information. As much as I loved this nigga, he was the most evil and ruthless nigga I knew. Despite my thug shit and gang ties, deep down inside, I still had a heart for shit I chose to have a heart for. I think I got that good side from my ol' girl, cause this nigga Scar was all fucked up but I wasn't gon' sit here and argue with him about his business and how he chose to run it.

"You know what? You right." I waved the white flag. "You do you and I'ma do me. I'm out."

"I expect to see you for Christmas breakfast. Don't disappoint yo' mama." He reminded me as I walked off.

This nigga had pissed me off in the worst way. "Yeah, I'll be here."

"Snow!" He called out. "I see that look in yo' eyes son. Don't do shit you might regret later. Let's just keep everything smooth like it's been."

His words fell on my back right along with deaf ears. I'd be less of a man to know Mani's story and not do shit about it. If it started a war between blood, then so be it. I didn't even tell my ol' girl bye or nothing. I hopped in my truck, pulled off, and called Reece letting him know I needed to holla at him. If nobody had my back, I knew he did, and it was time to round up a good solid niggas to help me get the job done. The same money I would've paid Scar for him to sell her to me, I was gon' use that money to pay these ruthless niggas and one thing about it; money talked bullshit walked.

Chapter Ten
Chantel

"Come on baby, it's been weeks and you still refuse to touch me. Don't you think it's about time that we made love? You don't miss me?" I whined as I straddled Dru wearing nothing besides a thong. Although Scar was dicking me down, it wasn't the same as with Dru. Sex with Dru was more passionate. Where Scar fucked me, Dru made love to me and I had an itch that really needed some scratching. I wanted Dru to scratch it all night long, but he refused to even kiss me. He stared at the blank flat screen television that was mounted up on our living room wall. He had a bottle of Don Julio in one hand and a joint in the other. As handsome as he is, he hadn't gotten a haircut in weeks and barely even left the house. It seemed like he was a totally different man then the one I'd known all of this time.

Had I known that getting Mani taken was going to cause such a strain on even our sex life, I probably would've reconsidered. I expected for him to be solely dependent on me for emotional support and this would made us stronger. I needed to know that had anything happened to him I would get everything that belongs to him and not Mani. She couldn't get shit if she was dead and gone. The fact that he was so torn up over her really made my stomach do flips. He didn't need her! I was all the woman he needed! That little bitch was just always in the way and was too damn expensive. "I miss my fuckin' daughter Chantel. That's who I miss. You think I have time to be worried about some pussy? You think ion notice that you haven't once acted like this shit has affected you just as much as it affects me? Move…" He gently pushed me off of him so he could stand up. I tripped over my damn self and stumbled on the floor causing a soft thud.

I stood up going after him with my ass cheeks and titties bouncing right along with me. "Wait hold the fuck up. You don't know shit. Maybe I just show emotions a little differently but that doesn't mean that I don't give a fuck Dru! Stop trying me like I'm some kind of evil ass bitch." I spat.

He brought the bottle up to his mouth and took a swig. When he gulped it down, he hit the joint and released a cloud of smoke before he blankly stared at me. Dru still had money, but with no crew, he put a complete halt on his operation for now. "Did I say that?" He asked.

"Well, you're insinuating it." I huffed slowly walking up on him placing each of my hands on his shoulders before massaging them. "I know it's a messed-up situation baby but being this way toward one another isn't going to bring her back. I wish she was still alive too." As soon as I said those words, I regretted it. Dru spun around with anger flickering in his eyes. Next thing I knew, he was grabbing me by my neck lifting me from the floor. My feet were dangling up under me and I was trying to scratch at his hands. He looked like a soulless nigga glaring at me.

"Bitch don't be so quick to write my fuckin' daughter off. Just cause the streets says she dead, don't mean she's dead. I know how this shit goes. If I know any better, I'll say that someone is trying real hard to make her disappear, that's why I haven't been able to get no information yet. That nigga Scar is dead, and I'ma make sure of it without a fuckin' army. He takes something from me, I'ma take something from him… his mu'fuckin' life. Timing is everything." He growled releasing me as the tears welled up in my eyes. He looked at me with disgust in his eyes. "I'm not so out of my element that I didn't smell the scent of another nigga when you walked in here the other day… and you wonder why I won't fuck you? Fuck outta my way." He stepped over me leaving me holding my neck with burning tears. Dru had never so much as cursed at me so I knew damn well this was causing him to lose his damn mind. A few moments later, I heard the front door slam letting me know that he was leaving, something he rarely did so I knew he was leaving to get the fuck away from me. I couldn't have my husband treating me like this. He needed closure if we were going to get our relationship back on track.

Hopping up from floor, I rushed to shower in the guest bathroom and then threw on some long jeans with my Steve madden boots. I found a hoodie and some mittens to put on, grabbed a few wads of money from my safe, and rushed out of the house. I needed to get to the Brothel ASAP and I knew that Scar probably wasn't there this time of evening, which was perfect. Instead of diving the Bentley, I hopped in my Jeep Wrangler and sped off. On the way, I stopped by Walgreens and grabbed a Trac phone. When I pulled up to the Brothel, my tires nearly burned rubber when I came to a screeching halt. I had a shank under my seat that I also kept as a part of my own protection. Grabbing that as well, I hopped out and made my way inside. I was met by Chico. "What you doin' here tonight? We weren't expecting you."

"I know. I need to see Bird. Like now."

"She's with a client."

I sucked my teeth. "Well, have one of them niggas to get that nigga up outta there because this is business also."

He shook his head. "Nah, you know we can't do that. She got about another thirty minutes so you can chill. Want a drink?"

Chico was about to piss me off but logically thinking, I had no right to be. Business was business and I couldn't intervene here. Besides, if Scar heard about it, I'd never hear the end of it. "Let me get some Fireball." I reluctantly replied while dragging my feet over to the bar. Chico wasn't talking about shit that I wanted to hear but I had to chill to let this little time pass. When I was done, her client was leaving, and I finally made it on the third floor to her room. When I walked in, Bird had one leg hiked up on the nightstand wiping her bare pussy with a wipe. "That's what the bathrooms are for Bird."

She rolled her eyes and got back to what she was doing. "On God, those shits are always occupied so in the meantime, I have to do this until one is free. What you doin' here?"

I made sure the door was closed all the way and then leaned up against the wall. I pulled out the wads of money from my purse and tossed them on the bed along with the shank and the Trac phone. "It's time."

Her eyes lit up landing on the money but was confused about everything else. "Time for what?"

"Remember I asked you if you ever killed anyone? I asked you to come here to make some bread and get close to Mani so she can trust you."

She raised a brow and stop wiping herself. Dropping her leg, she walked over to the bed and fold her arms across her bare breast. "Okay... and?"

"And it's time. It's imperative that she is gone for good. You gon' have to get it done some time this week. I don't know how you can get away with it, but it needs to be done quick and smooth within' this week. Make it look like y'all had some kind of disagreement or something."

"And then what?" She asked.

"And then nothing bitch. What do you mean? Carry on with your life."

"And why couldn't you get one of these other hoes in here to do it? I know you told me, but I don't remember what the fuck you said so run that by me again."

"I don't trust them not to tell Scar what the real deal was because these hoes have built different relationships with him... that's why. Any more questions?"

"How much is this?" She eyeballed the money picking one of the wads up forking through it with her finger.

"That's ten."

She shook her head. "Not enough for me to catch a body, bitch. Make it ten more."

"After the job is done."

"Humph…" She flopped down on the bed and picked up the trac phone. "And the phone?"

"You're gonna need it to call me and keep me updated on what's going on. My number is in there. Hide the damn phone too, Bird. Don't get caught with it. They don't want you hoes having a phone for a reason."

She rolled her eyes. "Whatever. I'll call you when it's done. Are we done here? I need to go actually wash my ass for real and pray like hell one of the bathrooms are free."

I nodded my head. "Yeah, we're done."

I walked out, hoping that she didn't fuck this up for me because I simply couldn't afford anymore fuck ups. On the way home, I drove through Da Towers just to see what was popping tonight. I had no intentions on getting out. I just simply tried to kill time before going home. I didn't even know how to face Dru right now and it was eating me up. I had no recruits to take to the Brothel and since Scar was probably home with his wife, he couldn't entertain me either. That was my problem. I seek attention because I never got it growing up and when I did, it was the wrong kind of attention. I hated to be alone and whenever I was put in a position to, it made me panic. I couldn't have Scar because he would never leave Michelle for me, or anybody else for that matter. Dru on the other hand, he was mine. I know I may have done some fucked up shit that I still hadn't spoken about till this very day, but I'd die trying to keep my secrets. I couldn't lose Dru because he was all I had. When I finally did make it home, Dru was back so instead of going in, I had to gather my thoughts. Pulling of a Grabba leaf from my purse, I rolled me a joint and sat in the car smoking it just thinking about all the shit that I'd been through in life. I'm a money hungry, selfish ass bitch and I knew that. No matter how much I prayed on it, I knew I would never change. Shit, nobody tried to change their life to be better people to me so fuck it. This shit was fair game in a lot of ways. When you've seen what I've seen, you end up like this. People could say what they wanted about me, but they couldn't have survived the shit I been through.

Chapter Eleven
Mani

I couldn't stop thinking about Snow since he left that day and honestly he gave me hope. His words soothed me in a way that nobody had been able to do these past weeks. My days went by easier and I had managed to stay off of Scar's bad side. I had just finished entertaining one of my regular weirdos. He had a foot fetish and he didn't want shit besides to rub my feet while he told me about his issues at his job and complained about his wife. He could talk for hours and I'd act like I was listening for hours even giving my input from time to time although I didn't know what the hell I was talking about. Nor did I give a damn about his wife or his job. The only thing that made me happy was the fact that I didn't have to fuck him.

When his time was up, I was escorted to the powder room to get touched up before my last client for the night. It was almost dinner time and I was starving. I was so glad to see that I was the only girl in the powder room right now because I didn't trust none of these females and the only one I was down with having a little conversation with was Bird. Lorraine was talking to one of Scar's men outside of the door while I waited for her. When she walked in, she gave me a genuine smile. "How you been little Ms. Bella?"

"I hate that, you know I do."

"I know baby… I'm sorry, I was just trying to lighten up the mood. Wrong choice of words." She apologized. "How you doing baby girl?"

"I'm okay I guess." I mumbled. "Just needed to freshen up."

Before she could say anything else, Bird came walking in like she was in a rush or either panicking. She had this wild look on her face. "Mani!" She squealed when she saw me. Catching me off guard she wrapped both of her arms around me nearly knocking me out of the chair when she hugged me. I sat frozen wondering what the hell was going on. "I've been looking everywhere for you!"

"Bird, what's wrong?" I asked.

She pulled some money from her bra and gave it to Lorraine. "Listen, I need a favor. Can you please excuse us for five minutes? I just need to have a personal conversation with Mani and I need the little man at the door to be distracted. We don't get no privacy around here."

Lorraine eyeballed the money. "You know I'm not supposed to do this, but I'll give you five minutes. Hurry up." She walked out and closed the door leaving us alone while she went to distract him.

"Mani listen, you have to find a way to get the fuck out of here. Like as soon as possible okay? Now I know you're going to hate me for this but when I came here, my motive was for more money and to live luxurious for a while. Chantel recruited me and she wanted me to get close to you just to…" She sighed. "Ya know, get next to you and shit.

114

You know what? I'm not even about to beat around the bush. The bitch wanted you to trust me so it wouldn't be hard for me to get next to you to kill you."

I gasped. "Kill me?!" I nearly jumped out of my seat but she quickly grabbed me by both of my shoulders forcing me to sit back down.

"Relax Mani. I don't want to hurt you. From the minute I found out how old you were, it made me realize what kind of sick, evil bitch I was dealing with. I don't fuck with her like that but she doesn't know it."

My eyes clouded with tears. "So you were supposed to kill me? All of these conversations and acting like you were looking out for me and that shit was fake?"

"Wasn't no acting. I fuck with you forreal Mani, or else I wouldn't be risking myself to come and tell you what's going on. I just know it's not safe for you here. If I don't do it she'll find a way to do it. You have to go." She pulled out a small shank from her little pouch and gave it to me. "I don't know what to tell you besides keep this on you but don't get caught with it. At least it's some kind of protection."

"Times up." Lorraine announced walking back inside. As soon as she did. The lights went out. "What the hell?" Lorraine mumbled.

"Um Lorraine, what's going on?" I asked.

"The power went out," said Bird.

Before anyone of us could regroup and adjust, gunfire begin to rang out all throughout the mansion. The screams coming from the hallways and the other floors made it sound like we were in the middle of the movie 'Scream' that's how loud it was. The security at the door held on to his little flashlight and opened the door.

"Stay here!" He yelled before leaving us.

"Lorraine!" I yelled since I couldn't see her.

"I'm right here little one! I'm right here." She followed my voice until she was holding my trembling hand. Bird found her way over to us next.

"Lorraine ya'll getting robbed and we gon' die!" Bird yelled. "What the fuck is goin' on and why the fuck would the nigga with the gun leave us in here without shit!"

I used my free hand cupping it over my mouth trying not to scream. This shit gave me flashbacks in the worst way. It took me back to the night I got kidnapped. "Not again." I whispered and cried at the same time. I tried to tune the gunshots out but the louder they rang out let me know it was getting closer to us.

"This shit is worse than the 'Wild Wild West'…" Bird was going on and on. The door bust open causing us all to jump. We clung on to each other as the flashlight bounced around our faces. It was Big Bird.

"Come on!" He yelled for us to come out. "I gotta get ya'll out of here. It's a mu'fuckin' ambush!" I had never in my life been so happy to see his ass. We all hopped up and ran out following his lead. He made us stay close behind him as he aimed his gun in front of him ready to use it. It was still a lot of activity but it was even darker in the hallways. We made it to the end of the hall to the staircase and followed each other down. As soon as we reached the first floor, I saw the outside lights shining through the front door. I clung on to Big Bird from behind and wanted to scream at all of the glass ripping into my bare feet since I wasn't wearing any shoes. I barely had on clothes and neither did Bird. We both had on lingerie and robes.

With the help of the outside light from the door, I was able to see multiple niggas dressed in all black shooting. It was niggas popping up from behind the bar, behind the couches, and from behind the walls. Big Bird snatched away from me and shot aimlessly into the living room not giving a fuck who he hit. I could see the reddish orange sparks flying from the many different kinds of guns. Just as quick as Big Bird ran off, he took one to the chest and I watched in horror as his heavy body hit the floor. The crimson red blood seeped from underneath him. I involuntarily scream aloud in horror. Something else was wrong. My hands were empty, I hadn't even realized that I got separated from Lorraine and Bird. They must've ran for cover and here my dumb ass was stuck in the middle of a warzone ducking and dodging bullets.

I was stuck, but I knew I had to try to make a run for it. Ignoring the pain in my feet, I took off to the front door. It was so close I could grab the knob. In a matter of seconds, I was being pulled from behind my hair. I couldn't see who it was but the grip he had on my hair hurt like hell as I screamed for someone to please help me. I felt as though my heart was going to bust out of my chest.

I swear I heard a bullet whisp right above me and then suddenly my hair was let go and I fell to the floor in pain. Once again, I forced myself to try to get up and this time, I was lifted in the air by another mask man who ran me outside while the other niggas who were still in the living room having a shootout covered him. "Let me go!" I kicked and screamed finally begging as I was ran out to an awaiting black Escalade with extremely dark tints. In my mind, I knew it was over for me. Chantel had found a way to get rid of me for good. He tried to toss me inside but I fought really hard until the gunshots followed us outside and a bullet whisp past my head again.

I didn't fight when I was forced in this time. I fell over when the driver hit the gas the peeled off. The screeching tires confirmed that we were moving even when my brain was slow on registering what was happening right now. Bullets bounced off of the truck while I ducked and closed my ears. The mask man rolled down the window, aimed a huge AK-47 out of the backseat window and let it rip. I didn't know where the hell I was going or who I was with. I just prayed these niggas didn't kill me. Once again, I was in a fucked up position. I didn't get up until the shooting stopped. "Get up shorty."

My head shot up. "Huh?"

He took the mask off and stared at me. A visible line of blood ran down the side of his face. Those eyes: the same eyes I could never forget stared down at me. He didn't look as calm as he looked before. Right now, he looked like a stone cold killer. His face was hard but yet softened up a little when he looked me in the eyes realizing how afraid I was. My silk robe was wet with fresh blood and my feet were bleeding real bad from the shattered pieces of glass stuck in them. "Snow? What the hell?" I couldn't believe he was here right on front of me.

"I told you to trust me right? Ain't nobody gon' hurt you again Mani. Get up." He ordered again. I slowly tried to get up and sat on the seat. He pulled out a smaller gun. "You know how to shoot?"

"No.... no." I stuttered.

"You gon' learn today. Pay attention." He released the clip and then quickly showed me where the safety was, how to cock, shoot and etc. "Now here, hold on to this until we get to where we're goin' and if anybody gets behind us, you shoot; I mean it, try to blow a nigga head off."

Oh Lord. I thought to myself. My life had never been this crazy and it made me realize how much of my protector that my daddy really was because he covered my eyes to a lot of dark shit in this world. I clung on to the gun hoping that I didn't have to use it. However, I still couldn't allow myself to get too comfortable around him just yet. If I had to, I'd use it on him too.

Chapter Twelve
Mani

I'm not sure where we were when we stopped, but it was behind a sixteen floor building. The truck came to a screeching halt. There were more Escalades pulling up shortly after us and niggas with mask hopped out wearing all black. Snow reached in the back of the seat and grabbed a big coat to put over me. After he slid out, he grabbed me in a cradle position and carried me through the building and up a flight of stairs although there was an elevator right there. I felt like I wanted to pass out, but at the same time, I felt good in his arms. Some of the niggas stayed behind, some walked in front of us with their guns out and some walked behind us. I also clung on to the gun he gave me. I didn't know shit about Snow, but this right here showed me that he must really be somebody special. I couldn't believe he came and got me up out of there. Even still, I was smart enough to know that this was far from over. I tried to ignore the cold air that smacked my entire body. The coat was helping, but it wasn't doing much justice, especially with the blood on me, it made it worse.

Snow carried me all the way up to the sixteenth floor and when he got in front of a burgundy door, a female opened it and let us in. She looked like she was in her twenties, maybe mid-twenties. "Damn, she okay?" She asked stepping to the side letting us in.

"Yeah, run some hot bath water for me True." He ordered her.

Nodding her head, she rushed off and did as she was told. He didn't let me out of his arms even while he waited. The dude standing next to him finally pulled off his mask. "You good nigga? Cause we ain't goin' nowhere. The snipers out over-time tonight." He pointed to the roof and I didn't know what that meant.

"Yeah Reece." He replied. "We need that fa'sho. Give me a minute." He told him while he walked me to the back where the bathroom was. True was just coming out of the bathroom. Her eyes bounced from mine to his. I didn't know who she was or her importance to him but she was really pretty.

"It's ready." She let him know.

"You can't put me down on my feet Snow. I have pieces of glass stuck in both feet."

"Let me see." True said bending down to take a look. "Oh it's bad too, it's a lot Snow."

"Well can you get it out?" He asked.

She gave him a sideway look. "Un Un it's too much and some of those pieces look deep as hell. She may even need a few stitches so you gon' have to call Doc." She informed. Again, I didn't know who the hell none of these people were that they were talking about.

Snow took a deep breath and exhaled. "Aiight look, I'm gon' put you down on the couch first and let Doc come take care of that real quick."

I simply nod my head. He took the gun from my hand and sat it on the coffee table before putting me down. I was still nervous but not as bad as before. If he wanted to kill me he wouldn't have done all of this. At the same time, this was truly bittersweet because I didn't ask him to come save me. He ruined the only chances I had of getting to my daddy with a clear tab for himself so we could go back to our happy lives 'after' I told him about Chantel's bitch ass. Deep down inside, I wished I was a cold blooded killer because I'd kill her without any hesitation. Now wasn't the time for me to express my frustration without seeming as if I'm being ungrateful though.

Snow stepped outside with Reece, meanwhile, I lay on my back staring at the ceiling. The girl True was still inside with me but she didn't ask any questions. She sat at the table smoking a hookah. The apartment was nice and cozy, much different from the outside of the building which didn't look like much and wasn't very welcoming at all. It was made of reddish colored bricks and that's about it.

Next time the door opened up, Snow was coming back inside with an older woman. She was very bright skinned with a face full of pimples. Covering her eyes were an extremely huge pair of prescription glasses. She looked welcoming though, she didn't look mean at all.

"This is Doc." Snow told me. "She's gon' get yo' feet cleaned up and get that glass out of there so you can get in the tub."

I nodded my head letting him know I was okay with that. Snow excused himself out of the door again, and this time, True followed. Doc focused on me pulled out all kind of shit from her bag. She didn't even look like a damn doctor to me at all. "Are you a real doctor?" I asked.

She pulled up a stool and smirked. "If that's what you want to call it. I got all the way to the end of medical school before I got locked up. I took a charge for my baby's daddy so he wouldn't get locked up and that same charge got me ten years. I couldn't find good work after that so these niggas call me when they need me and they pay me good."

I frowned. "So do you know what you're doing?" I needed to know because she was about to freak me out. She wasn't even a real doctor and Snow had her up in here playing with my damn feet as if I didn't ever plan on walking again.

She smirked. "I know enough… listen don't move. I'm going to shoot some of this in both of your feet to numb them a little and it may pinch just a little bit."

"Okay…" I agreed. She was right, it did pinch a little bit but it wasn't bad. It sure did numb me up some too because my feet no longer hurt to the extreme. I didn't have the energy to talk to her much. Every so often Snow would peek his head inside to take a look and then pop his head right back out. As I lay here it dawned on me. Once again, I was put in a position of not even knowing where I was. I decided to ask Doc. "Where am I?"

"Did I ask you what happened to your feet, or about the blood all over your robe?" She asked. It wasn't in a rude tone or nothing though.

"No."

"Okay then hunny. That's how it is around here. We don't meddle or get in people's business. Anything you want to know you have to ask Snow since he's the one that brought you over here to the jungle."

Jungle? I thought to myself. I didn't say shit else to her. My thoughts went to Bird and Lorraine. I'm not sure if they made it out. I wasn't sure if they were hurt or what was going on with them and I prayed that they were okay. We should've never been separated. We should've done better sticking with each other but at the same time I understood in the heat of the moment, every man was for themselves trying to stay safe and keep a bullet from ripping through their asses. "You're all done and you have a few dissolving stitches but I also applied medical glue over them as a sealant so the stitches won't be affected if you shower and stuff. It'll be real sore to try to walk for the next few days but eventually it'll get better. You can take Tylenol for the pain if it gets too bad."

"Thank you." I replied. I didn't feel shit right now because the numbing shot she gave me was still working. She called Snow inside and let him know that she was done. She also let him know that she had a few crutches in her apartment and she would bring back two for me. In return, he gave her a knot of money before she went on her way. True was no longer with him either. However, I did hear deep voices on the other side of the door.

"How it feel?" He asked sitting across from me in the loveseat.

"It's still numb."

He slowly nod his head. He still hadn't cleaned up the trail of blood trickling down the side of his face, but I guess he wasn't too concerned with himself right now. "Good." He replied. Snow definitely stood out like a sore thumb. He was special and I felt it.

However, I couldn't hold back anymore. "Snow, do you know what you did? The man you stole me from is very dangerous and he's just downright ruthless. If he finds out who took me or where I am, it's going to be trouble. I'm not done paying off my debt." I explained with tears cascading down my face now. Although Bird dropped a bomb on me, and I probably would've had to leave anyway, I still needed to figure my own shit out. It didn't need to be done like this because this made it worse. I hadn't been crying before, but this conversation surely activated the tears because I just couldn't catch a break. "I just know this isn't over."

Snow was looking at me deeply. His demeanor didn't break either, which let me know he wasn't scared of anything, not even of what I was telling him. "I need to tell you somethin' that I didn't tell you before shorty, and I didn't not tell you cause I was tryna keep secrets; I didn't tell you cause you wouldn't have trusted me if did and I needed you to."

I gave him a side way look because I didn't know what he was coming at me with. I felt my heart pounding again. "What is it?"

"Ain't no way else to say it and I'm not the one to cut corners and shit so I'mma just say it. I know all about the man who owns the Brothel and what I'm up against. I've been knowing him all my life shorty. He's my ol' boy and I just went against him in a major way to get you up out of there. I tried to do it the right way and offered to pay yo' debt. In return he told me you wasn't for sale and he never planned on lettin' you go no matter what the situation. It wasn't no amount of money he's willin' to take from me or nobody else to save you. You became one of his top girls and his own greed didn't give a fuck about you or yo' life. So now that it's out, you can make a choice. I'll let you leave out of here right now, but you probably won't last a full day out there. It's up to you."

I couldn't believe this beautiful man in front of me was telling me that he was the product of something so ugly. Snow may have been dangerous in his own way, but the fact that he did this to save me even when he could've gotten himself killed, showed me his heart. As mad as I wanted to be at him for not disclosing that information at first, I understand why he did what he did. Had he told me that, I would've never entertained any kind of conversation with him but it all made sense as in to why he was even at Scar's anniversary party. "So his wife…"

He cut me off. "Yeah, that's my ol' girl and nah she ain't shit like him."

"I take it you and Scar don't get along?"

"We aiight. I love my pops. Nigga taught me everything I know."

I was so confused by this whole ordeal. I just didn't understand why he would do that to his blood. I sighed and shook my head. "Why Snow? Just tell me why because I'm not understanding why you went against him tampering your relationship for me?"

"Look shorty, somebody had to show the nigga he's not untouchable. Why not it be me? I gotta be one of the only niggas that's not scared of the man. At some point, somebody gotta calm his ass down. I don't know what yo' life mean to you, but obviously it means somethin' to me." He told me as he stood back up. My eyes followed him. "I gotta get True so she can help you to the tub ma."

"No, why can't you do it?" I asked.

"Because, then I'll have to strip you naked and then put you in the tub."

"And?" I asked wondering what the problem was. "You ain't never seen pussy before? True can't carry me Snow."

"I mean, you seventeen shorty, until you turn at least eighteen, I'm not tryna be involved with none of that." He let me know just as there was a knock on the door. He excused himself and then grabbed the two crutches from Doc before bringing them over to me. "Look, she was right on time to save me the debate. You can use these and take yo'self and then I'll send True to help you out."

The more he spoke, the more I liked him beyond his looks. Lately, I hadn't had any men actually giving a fuck about respecting me and then here he comes being the perfect gentleman and even taking my age into consideration. "I can respect that."

"Any more questions?" he asked as he removed one of his guns from is waist sitting it on the table in front of him. He then walked to the blinds and peeked downstairs. He pulled a walkie from his pocket. "Yo, I need this door to be secure at all times," he told the dude who answered it. He let Snow know he was on it before Snow returned his attention back to me. "Questions?" He asked again.

"Where am I?"

"Da Towers." He replied. I raised a brow.

"The projects." He further explained.

"Um okay and will I be safe here? Will 'You' be safe here?"

"Nobody's untouchable ma, but this is the safest place for you and me both right now. This ain't an easy building to get into. Can't no random just walk up in this building. We know everybody who lives here and we know all the faces of mu'fuckas who come over here to visit those same people. Some shit look fishy, the snipers on the roof gon' light this shit up before a nigga foot can hit the sidewalk." *Snipers on the roof?* I thought. Now I knew what they were talking about earlier.

I sighed feeling a wave of sadness come over me, at the same time, I was anxious. "Why didn't you just take me to my daddy? I mean, you said he's still alive right?"

"I can't do that Mani. As soon as they realize that you're gone; where's the first place you think they gon' stalk out? If you wanna see yo' daddy alive? For now you gotta chill and stay far away from him until it's time."

I didn't like the sound of that, but I did understood where he was coming from. I adjusted the crutches under my arm pits so I could go to the bathroom. It wasn't until I did that did I realized that I still couldn't hop to the bathroom. "You know what? To prevent myself from becoming too paranoid, I'd rather revisit this conversation later; for now though, I just realized I still can't take myself because it's not like I can hop on just one foot so you're still gon' have to take me."

Snow took a moment to look me up and down before he realized that I was right. "Damn shorty." He chuckled. "You right."

"Um Hmm."

Ditching the crutches, he once again lifted me into his arms and then sat me on the toilet so he could drain the water and make some new water since the previous water had gotten cold. When he was done, he told me, "I'ma go get True so she can help you now. You can start takin' that shit off." I watched his broad shoulders as he walked away. His presence was so strong, it was hard to not be drawn to him.

I took the robe off followed by my bra. I removed the lace panties that I had on next and then carefully, I used the heel of my feet to drag myself into the warm water. When it hit my body, I felt like I was in paradise. The hot water targeted every single part of my aching body bringing a smoothness to it that was much needed. I closed my eyes and let my head rest for a few minutes and when I opened them it's because I felt someone

standing over me. There was True just looking.
"Hey," I mumbled.

"Hey," she replied finally breaking our stare down so she could grab some shampoo and Epsom salt from under the sink. She opened the bag and slowly poured some into the water. Next, she used a cup to wet my hair before cupping one of her hands and filling it with shampoo so she could wash my hair. I couldn't even appreciate this moment because all it did was made me think back to the Brothel, we got pampered just like this and while most people would love it, I was over it. However, that didn't have shit to do with True so I couldn't take it out on her by being a bitch. After she washed my hair, she let out the now blood filled water and replaced it with some fresh water and more Epsom salt. "You need me to wash you up?

"Nah, I got it. I can do it." I refused to let her wash me up. I wasn't handicap and I didn't want to be treated like it. I decided that when I got out, I was walking on my own. I didn't care if I had to use the heel of my feet to do it in order to avoid the pain.

She dried her hands and nodded her head. "Okay, in the room across the hall there's some stuff on the bed that you can put on. Your dry off towel is right here." She pointed to a folded u towel she had placed on the counter.

"Thank you." I mumbled. "I got it from here." I told her. Even then, she still hadn't moved to leave. She was back staring at me as if she was examining my whole being. "What?" I asked.

"You know… you're very pretty."

"Thank you... so are you."

She lightly smiled. "Thank you." She responded still not moving. I lathered up the rag and begin washing myself. "Sooo you're just gon' stare?"

"My bad, I'm just daydreaming in my own thoughts. You know, Snow likes yo' lil young ass."

"Young?" I frowned. "You don't even know how old I am."

"Oh, don't take it offensive. I just know you're younger than me. I'm twenty-five."

I nodded my head. "Ohh okay, well yeah I'm younger than you and how would you know how Snow feels? Because he looked out for me? He's probably a protector of women."

"Yeah, okay." She laughed. "I know what I see in his eyes when he looks at you."

"How would you know that look unless you're busy looking and trying to read him?" I asked. See, I was smart enough to peep shit as well.

She shrugged. "It is what it is. I've been knowing Snow for a minute now and this situation right here is the most devoted time he's given any female. I mean, I could be wrong, but I'm probably right."

The entire time she spoke, I read her eyes and her body language. "You like him don't you?"

"Sometimes." She told me with the wink of an eye. "However, right now all that doesn't matter. We're one big family around here and we all look out for each other. Snow called me over here cause he knows I'm loyal and I don't run my mouth. I'll be heading home in a few."

"So this isn't your apartment?" I asked.

"Nope, this is just a spare that Snow uses for any occasion. It's nice in here huh?"

"Yeah, I guess." I replied yawning. My stomach growled from the lack of eating anything but at the same time, I didn't have an appetite. True finally excused herself and when she did, I got out of the tub and walked on my heels until I reached the room she was referencing. Laid out on the bed was a bottle of lotion, some body spray, a white t-shirt and a pair of long spandex. After I used everything and put it on, I used the towel to dry my own hair and the braided it back in one big French braid. I heard someone else coming through the front door and was relieved when I saw Snow standing there, which was good, because I needed to know the plan moving forward.

Chapter Thirteen
Snow

While Mani was getting situated, I was making sure everything was set up how it needed to be. I planned on staying here one night only. Simply because I didn't want to chance going home tonight and leave shorty behind, that wasn't an option. Although nobody knew where I lived, it was the principle of the matter. A nigga rather had been safe than sorry. I made sure that the building was locked down meaning nobody comes in and nobody leaves out tonight. Leaning up against the wall, I passed a joint to Reece. This door would be guarded all night. "You know Scar gon' be mad about that nigga Chico. I know he gotta be dead. Ain't no way that nigga survived that. He took a hit straight to the heart."

"We knew what this shit was gon' be like before we went in. Chico got popped and we lost a soldier too." I replied thinking about my nigga Skip. I didn't even want Skip to go, but he was one of those wild hot head niggas that didn't give a fuck about life. Skip wasn't scared to die under no circumstances. He lived by the gun and he died by the gun. "Tomorrow, I want you to take his ol' girl his cut of his money. Give her my number and let her know if she ever needs me she can call me."

Reece nodded his head agreeing. "You's one solid mu'fucka Snow… crazy, but Solid. Any nigga go up against Scar ain't got it all but I'ma ride wit'chu regardless nigga, you already know." He gave me a pound of the fist. "If anything ever happens to me, I want you to make sure everybody around here is still good." "I got'chu bruh, but let's be real, ain't shit gon' happen to you. Nigga you built to last." "Unlike that nigga Scar, I'm smart enough to know I'm not untouchable. You know how this shit go." "Trust me, you gon' be aiight." True walked out of the door holding her purse. "Well, she's in there getting dressed. I'm about to go home." "Aiight, appreciate that ma." I paid her. I had a habit of paying everybody for their services even when they didn't ask. Simply because I never wanted nobody holding shit over my head. Not even True.

She eyeballed the money. "Thank you…" I knew she wanted to say more, but with Reece standing right here she knew better. I didn't talk my personal business in front of mu'fuckas and anything I wanted him to know would come from my mouth. I watched her walk off and disappear. As soon as she was out of my presence, I received a page to call her. Right now, I didn't have time for that. I had bigger shit to worry about.

"You think True gon' be a problem?" Reece asked.

"Doubt it, but she's the only female around here that I could've trusted with Mani right now. You know these other bitches be on some other shit sometime."

He agreed with a simple nod of the head. Reece then went inside of his favorite duffle bag and pulled his burners out making sure the clips were fully loaded. The later in the night it got, the chillier it got. A page came through from an unrecognizable number and I had a feeling it was Scar. I pulled out one of the two trac phones that I had on me today and called the number back.

"Speak." I said into the phone as soon as somebody picked up.

"You left something behind lil nigga. If you want his body back, you bring me my property back."

"I'm not bringin' you shit Scar. I love you and all but you one sick mu'fucka. You took somethin' from me, and I took somethin' from you. A life for a life, you taught me that." I reminded him. He took a loss with Chico being dead and Da Towers took a loss with Skip being dead so as far as I was concerned. We were even.

"You sure you want to play with my money like this? You broke the rules Snow. Now daddy gon' have to teach you a lesson." He tried to taunt me but it wasn't working.

"Whatever the fuck it's gon' be then that's what it is. I'm not bringin' shorty back. Ion know what the fuck to tell you. She ain't have no business there in the first place."

He sighed, "Snow, you crossed me over some pussy. I would've given you any pussy up in here that you would've asked for, just not that pussy."

This nigga had me throwed because he really had a control thing goin' on with shorty. By her being so young and tender, he knew that she could've given him a few years in the game to make him some real good money and that's all he gave a fuck about. "It's not about the pussy. I'm not fuckin' the girl. You say you taught me everything I know; you also taught me that greed could get'chu killed. Remember that Scar. Yo, dick might've help to bring me in this world, but I'm my own man and I ain't no bitch. Nobody's punking me. This shit an eye for an eye. We both lost two good soldiers today. You can leave this shit alone, or it's whatever."

"This shit is real Snow." He warned.

"I'm aware."

There was a long silent pause. I didn't know what Snow was thinking, but I knew he was up to something. Reece held his gun to his side and made sure that everybody else was in place. "It's a cold world out here Snow."

"I'm always dressed for the weather." I let him know before hanging up. I didn't have time to entertain Scar. He was so unpredictable that I couldn't even say he wouldn't really try to kill me; right now though, I couldn't be worried about that. I excused myself from with Reece and walked back inside. Mani looked like she had just got finished getting herself together. I laughed at the way she looked walking around on both of her heels but I guess she had to do what she had to do. Even fully covered in clothes, she was still pretty. "You hungry?" I asked.

She took a seat on the bed. "I don't really have an appetite." My eyes bounced around for the gun I'd given her. "I know this is new to you ma, but moving forward, I need you to have that gun close to you at all times."

"Snow, I'm afraid. I'm not even gon' lie. Like when something doesn't feel right it just doesn't feel right. I know Scar is coming for us, facts."

"One thing about life. We live just to die and we all gotta go one day. Trust me when I tell you that no matter what, I'm not gon' let shit happen to you."

She patted the empty spot on the bed next to her motioning for me to come and sit next to her. Reluctantly, I went. Even if I wanted to return shorty to Scar, I was in way too deep now. Mani didn't know it, but we were stuck like glue at this point. She was gon' be my wife, my rider, my everything and she didn't even know it. I had never said that shit or felt that about no female that I'd been around. Her past and what Scar had put her through didn't define her. She didn't let that shit take her soul. I didn't look at her like a nasty trick or no shit like that. If anything shorty was a fighter and she did what she had to do to survive. That shit didn't do nothing besides make her stronger. She was the real beast out here, she didn't realize how strong she was now because she hadn't been activated yet. When she realized it, it was gon' be over for a lot of mu'fuckas cause she would no longer deal with disrespect. "It's not just about me Snow. I'm concerned about the other two people that were with me before we got separated and I don't want shit to happen to them."

"Who?" I asked with furrowed brows.

"Well one of them is our house mom Lorraine, and the other one is this girl named Bird."

I realized that she was unaware of who Lorraine really was. Now Bird, that was another story. I sighed. "Look, I know who Bird is aiight, cause she's from here and I also know that she's as tough as they come. I'm sure she's good."

"And Lorraine?"

Once again, I took a deep breath. I hated to keep disappointing this girl, but I couldn't sit here and lie to her. Seemed like that's all she'd been getting fed was lie after lie. "Ain't nothin' gon' happen to Lorraine shorty. I hate to be the one to tell you this but Lorraine is my auntie. She's good."

I didn't know what to expect from her hearing that but it wasn't a look of surprise or disappointment. I could tell she was just over it. "Wow." She softly replied.

"So she's Scar's sister?" She asked.

"It's complicated ma, cause she's my ol' girl's sister too."

Mani just shook her head, "please spare me the details. I think I'mma be sick, like this dead ass makes a person like me not trust anybody at all."

"Nah, Lorraine is good people. It's just a crazy situation."

"Yeah… okay."

"If you don't wanna eat shit, I think you need to get some rest."

Staring into my eyes, she had that look in hers that once again made me want to protect her. I pulled her into my arms and laid back on the bed with her. If she didn't feel security anywhere else, I hoped she felt it right here. Our breathing was on the perfect cue with each other's. The rhythm of our beating hearts were beating in the rhythm of one. I laid here in silence with her head rested on my chest deep in our own thoughts. When she finally went to sleep, I gently removed her from my arms and lay her head on the pillow before placing a blanket over her body. I got up and sat in the chair directly in front of the bed and watched her looking like sleeping beauty as she slept. I was glad I had some time to myself so I could put a play in motion. I didn't want her to worry about none of this shit. I'd been going in and out of the apartment for the rest of the night well into the wee hours of the morning. I had to make sure my niggas was good. As soon as I made it back inside, the pager was going off again, and this time I called back from another phone. "Speak."

"Look out of the window Snow." Scar instructed me damn near growling.

The fuck? I thought to myself. I pulled my 45mm from the small of my back and cocked it after making sure one was in the head. Slowly, I walked over to the window and barely cracked it back. Just enough to see. Parked across the street from Da Towers in an open field were five white bulletproof vans with black tints. I'd seen these vans before when I was younger. Scar never pulled these vans out unless he felt like someone was a real threat to him. The fact they I was staring at them let me know that even as his son, he didn't underestimate me.

"I see the punk ass niggas in the vans, so what'chu wanna do?" I growled.

"Let me get the lil bitch back and this can go away. You fuckin' with my money now you put me in position to fuck with yours."

I felt my nostrils flaring with the itch of my trigger finger. I breathed slow and steady wondering if this shit was even worth it. I briefly glanced at shorty peacefully sleeping. I knew the only reason she was even sleeping that peacefully is because I had assured her so many times that she could trust me and I wouldn't let anything happen to her. I didn't break my promises.

My mind was made up. "Nah, not an option so if you wanna play, let's play."

Scar let out a disappointing chuckle. "Aiight Snow, I tried to reason with you but fuck it… let the games begin lil one!"

I looked at Mani one more time wondering if she was 'G' enough to be ready for what was coming knowing that I'd just started a war with my own father… it was all in or nothing and I hoped she knew that. My name is Tray' Snow' mu'fuckin' Harris and if niggas didn't know, they was about to learn today!

To Be Continued…

Interested in keeping up with more releases from S.Yvonne? To be notified first of all upcoming releases, exclusive sneak peaks, and contest to win prizes. Please subscribe to her mailing list by texting Syvonnepresents to 22828 or by simply clicking here: Click Here To Subscribe

Please feel free to connect with me on social media as well:

Facebook: Author Syvonne Powell
Facebook: Author S.Yvonne
Facebook VIP Readers Group:
https://www.facebook.com/groups/5068827261
57516/?ref=share
Instagram: Authoress_s.yvonne

Made in United States
Orlando, FL
19 February 2023